VENGEANCE TRAIL
AZURE JAMES

© 2012 Azure James Gallagher Michalak. All rights reserved.

ISBN: 978-1-105-96766-5

Thank you!

My mom Amy Gallagher for her editing and story suggestions. My grandparents and great-grandparents, especially Grandma Ray and Sue. Michael LiVecchi, Mike Jackson and my dad for getting me experience in shooting. Casey Doss for being such an inspiring teacher to me, and also taking me shooting the first time. All my friends and family who donated or pre-ordered the book. My uncle Cory for draft reading. My horse-riding friends for all the fun times and inspiration!

VENGEANCE TRAIL

PROLOGUE
Wichita, Kansas, March 1, 1897:

Clint Patterson is my name. I was born in Wichita, Kansas, in 1875. Until recently, I lived in in Wichita, in a house I rented from my friends. I helped with odd jobs, repair work, and assisted Farmer Levin with his planting and harvesting. Life was good enough for me, although there seemed to be something missing.

However, on one rainy day, that changed. An important letter was delivered to me. It was from my father, who had moved to New Mexico several years before. I wondered what the letter could possibly be about, since my father and I had never been particularly close.

He explained to me in the message that he had a serious liver problem, and he didn't know how long he had to live. He wished to see me while he still had the chance. My father offered his old New Mexico cabin to me if I would go out West and visit him. It was quite a long and arduous journey.

I was unsure at first whether I wanted to go to New Mexico. However, after about a week, I made up my mind on the matter. Seeing my dad was a priority over my other plans. I knew that it was also important for him to see me, and for me to say goodbye if necessary. Also, it is not often that a person comes across an offer for a free house.

My wife Maddy took more convincing than me, but I did manage to persuade her to make the journey with me. We removed the lease on the house we were living in, and packed up the horses. We bought the cheapest wagon we could find from our neighbor Fred Windfall. I said goodbye to all my friends and neighbors, and to my mom. My mother and father had split up years before. They never told me exactly why, although I thought it was because my mother didn't want to go out West with my father. She was a mild and simple sort of person, and life on the frontier was too intense, violent, and rough for her.

We headed out from Kansas to New Mexico early in the spring of 1897. The trip was difficult, but I couldn't help but think of how much harder it had been for the pioneers fifty years before. They had no trails, companions, or supply stores on the way out West. The bumpy roads continued on for miles, slowly changing from prairie to brushy desert.

When we eventually arrived, my father was doing very poorly. The doctor had seen him, and he had only bad news. His lifetime of drinking and working had worn down his body. We stayed in the same house, although there was hardly enough room for three people in his small cabin.

My father and I had many talks about the past, about Kansas, and about New Mexico. He wished he'd moved back to Kansas. I told him it didn't really matter, since I got to see him while he was still around. We made our amends.

The situation became steadily more serious. I said my last goodbyes to my dad. I grieved his death for the rest of the spring. I wished I'd seen him more often after I left my parents' house. One fact did bring me comfort- my father had lived a long life considering all the work he'd done and all the fights he'd been in.

As time went by, my memory of him became less immediate and more distant. I began to focus more on trying to make a living in New Mexico. Maddy and I had a lot of pressing issues to sort out. It wasn't easy making our way in this crazy world.

As the summer of 1897 rolled around, I was starting to settle into life in the West. It was a far cry from the mundane Kansas life I had become used to. The people were not used to me being there, and I found there were a lot less towns and people than in Kansas. Farming was not easy there either, so the people had to make their living from other occupations. Most of all, there was a sense of wilderness and adventure in the air. New Mexico was hardly settled, and any people living there were in the first or second generation of settlers. On the other hand, Kansas had been farmed and settled for decades before I was even born.

CHAPTER 1
Raton, New Mexico, June 23, 1897:

Schwede's Saloon was the most popular place for a drink in Raton, mostly because it was the only real saloon in the whole town. There was an occasional bar fight or shootout there, but the main event was always bragging, gossiping, and storytelling. It was late in the afternoon. I had just finished helping the owner of the saloon fix up a room on the second floor. In return, I received a small wage and a few drinks.

The bar was made of dark stained walnut. The building was lit with a few gas lanterns, but they were not turned on, since it was only seven o'clock. The sun was a hand or two above the horizon, still yellow, but about to turn orange and then pink. Only a few other people were in the place. I knew them, even though I was just starting to get used to Raton.

"Hand me another round, Mister Martin," I said.

We had known each other since I first set foot in Raton, although we only seemed to talk about boring, mundane things. I felt like our friendship had progressed to the point where we could start getting to really know each other.

"If you don't mind me asking, what jobs did you have before you bought this bar?" I asked.
"Only one," replied Mister Martin. "I used to break and train them wild horses. There's an awful lot of them mustangs around here. I'll bet I broke at least three dozen of them over the years. But one of them kicked me in the side and broke my leg. Doctor said I almost died. Now I got this bad limp an' I can't do nothin' but look after this bar."
"That's too bad," I said sympathetically.
"Yes sir. What do you plan on doing? Are you gonna get a real job around here?" he probed.
"I ain't sure. I don't know if there are any jobs that are better than what I do already. It sure is hard to make a livin' around here. It ain't Kansas."

"You can't make much money offa' building stuff," said Mister Martin. "Maybe you should be a horse trainer like I was."

"I don't think so," I replied, doubtfully. "I can ride, but I can't rope or break. That's what you cowboys are for."

"I guess you're right, but how do you intend to get through the winter?" asked Martin.

"Hmm. I'm not too sure. It's been tough…and winter ain't even hit yet."

"We ain't got much food here. You'll have to make some good dollars before you buy any. That's why most of us try to grow a few plants and can food for the winter. I hope you don't die or nothin'. Winter over here ain't like it is in Kansas."

Martin was somber. I knew he spoke from experience. I began to worry. "I should have enough time to get myself some sort of good paying job by then. It's a while before winter anyways."

I overheard a few old locals whispering about me, not knowing I could hear them. Not many people in the town were used to me living there.

"You hear the Thompson Gang shot another innocent man yesterday… for no good reason at all?" said one of the men.

"Yep. Darned men deserve hangin' and shootin'. I can't stand them. Seems like they shoot people just like buffalo."

"That's for sure," replied the first man.

"But you know what? I don' like them people from the Midwest movin' in here. Like that Patterson man. He ruffles up our whole damn town! He don't belong here!" whispered someone gruffly.

"I know. There didn't used to be nobody from there back in the seventies. Heck, warn't even nobody here from Louisiana or Oklahoma back them, either. Just like that Gordon Mayford man."

"Quiet down." replied the second man. "That foreigner is in here right now. He might be spying on us."

I almost laughed, but I stopped myself just in time. The two men stopped whispering for a few minutes, and when they resumed, they talked about unimportant matters. Although I found it slightly offensive to be insulted in such a way, I knew there was nothing I could easily do to change the situation. It would take at least a year of living in New Mexico for the townspeople to like me much. Even though some of the younger men and women were quite friendly with me, it seemed the old men had some big problem with me being in town.

I decided I had drunk enough liquor for my liking. Besides, the owner of the bar only told me he'd give me two shots when I completed my job. I was too frugal to buy more. It was a good idea to save my money for food and good hay for the horses instead of alcohol.

I stood up and made my way towards the doors. The floor creaked like an old house. I swung them open. I took a final glance at the two old men, who were staring suspiciously at me.

Damn grouches, I thought. My chestnut gelding was waiting outside. A dark brown Quarter Horse, about fifteen hands high. He had a little white star on his forehead and a white sock on his left hind leg. I named him William after one of my old friends from Kansas.

William was rather impatient. He stomped at the ground and swished his tail. He looked at me when he saw me, and I could tell he was ready to leave the town.
"Let's go on home, William," I said to him.

I untied the reins from the hitching pole and walked to the near side of the horse. I put my left foot in the stirrup and hoisted myself on top of him. He backed up a few feet and started to bounce along forward at a steady trot.

After William had warmed up a bit, I tapped him with my right foot and he started to run a little faster down the trail out of Raton. The house was only about a forty minute ride away, and for that reason I went into town quite often. Not that people exactly enjoyed my presence there. On

5

the contrary, most of the locals were not standoffish and aloof. Still, being in the town is usually better than being constantly cooped up in the house.

My horse snorted happily. He really enjoyed running, so I thought I'd take him on a longer ride in the country. I steered him left off the dirt path, and Will started to canter through the bristly brush and dirt of the New Mexican badlands.

Because of the cacti, holes, and other possible dangers, I slowed him down to a moderate jog. There would be a good chance of finding a place where he could really stretch his legs soon, though.

We rode on for a long time, until we reached a vast plain without much brush to run in. I kicked my horse into a fast canter. The air blew through my hair, as I felt my horse roll back and forth under me. I stood up in the saddle a little bit, and held onto William's neck. I was lucky to have such an energetic horse. When I felt finished, I slowed William down. He wanted to run more, but I preferred to watch the spectacular desert sunset.

I observed the big orange sun go lower in the sky until it was right on the horizon. I reined Will up and dismounted. Then, I walked a few steps over to a big rock and sat on it. My horse was a few feet away from me.

The sky was bursting at the seams with colors: orange, red, pink, blue, and more. It was right halfway between day and night. I breathed slowly, tired from the long work day.

A cool breeze seemed to tell me I should hurry along, but the beautiful sunset made me sit a few more minutes. William walked around slowly and ate what few plants he could discover among the prickly cacti.

After watching the sun sink low in the sky, I mounted again and rode off to a big orange rock a few minutes away. I could just make out the path about two or three miles off in the distance.

"Don't worry, boy. We'll be headed back home soon."

We came up next to the big rock, and I looked up at it, amazed. I decided to go all the way around it, and get a closer look. I suddenly got a stomach cramp, so I slowed William down to a slow walk. Then, I saw something in the rock.

There was a certain piece of the orange rock formation that didn't look like it belonged where it was. Out of curiosity, I steered William towards it for a better look. On the edges of this large, flat, brown rock, I could see a little space. I knew it had to lead somewhere interesting. I was struck with a strange curiosity of the unknown. I got off William and tried to lift the rock up and move it.

It was very heavy, and it took all my strength to move the brown rock even a few inches. I kept slowly inching it away from the wall, and took a look inside. I saw a passageway heading straight underground.

My heart started to race a little bit, and I wondered what might be inside the passageway. I took a quick look outside to see if I had enough time to investigate before dark, but I wasn't sure. I already could hear the first cricket out in the distance, and it was growing darker by the minute.

I heard William whinny loudly, and saw him running away from something. I had no idea what he was so scared of, if anything. However, I knew William had keener senses than I. After shaking my head angrily, I chased after William, who had already run quite a distance away from me.

"Come on! Calm down. It's nothing. Let's get back to the house." I said.

I figured I could always head back to that rock later. If I went back and looked right then, my horse might spook again and get even farther away from me. Plus, night was falling quickly.

The two of us rode back to the trail just as thick darkness began to settle. Once I got back on it, I could eventually see my house light in the distance. I was just in time.

The ranch was small. We owned twenty acres of land, but the house itself only had three rooms. I spent a lot of my free time on the porch, since there wasn't very much to do inside the house.

I unsaddled William and put him in the barn. He was happy to be back home. After that, I fed him some hay and patted him before I went in the house. Even though William was at times a very temperamental and skittish horse, I still liked him for his endurance and general good nature. He had more personality than my wife's horse, Betty. I felt a sort of kinship with him, even though we were two entirely different species. I always thought horses were the closest to humans you can get without being one.

My partner Maddy was waiting for me in the house when I got there. "Happy you're home, honey… and you're not even stone drunk," she said with a laugh, and kissed my cheek. The ride in the country had helped me not to feel the liquor quite as much, and seeing her beautiful face brought me more to my senses.

CHAPTER 2
Raton, New Mexico, June 24, 1897:

Maddy was one of the prettiest girls in Kansas I ever did meet. Although I used to know of one girl slightly more beautiful than her, she was arrogant and snide. Nothing like my sweet wife. Maddy had long black hair, green eyes with hazel specks, and tan skin from riding and working outside. She was a few inches shorter than me, maybe five feet and six inches tall. She had a sweet and gentle demeanor. I'd met her three years before we moved to New Mexico. We were on our first anniversary of marriage. If I had ever made a mistake, it was not marrying her earlier. She had a heart of gold, and she was the best thing in my whole world.

The two of us had plans to invite our neighbor Mr. Josiah Tucker to breakfast, considering how lonely life can get in the desert, even with a partner to keep you company. Here we need all the friends we could get. We tried to get our neighbors over or go to their houses as often as we could. Maddy prepared the food, and I set the table. We were not wealthy enough to afford fancy food, but what we ate got the job done well enough. I heard a knock on the door. Josiah's face peered through the door-screen. I opened it and let him in.

Josiah Tucker was a medium-sized man, neither skinny nor overweight. He worked at the Raton Bank, as a teller and assistant to the manager, Paul Williams. Josiah had an abundance of black hair. He always wore a black flat-brimmed hat when outside. His face was slightly dirty, since it was one of his days off.

"How do you do, Josiah?" I asked.
"Very well, thank you. How are you?"
"Not too bad."
"And your wife?"
"I'm fine…" yelled Maddy, from the kitchen.
"Thank y'all for inviting me to breakfast. I ain't got enough places to go to."

"It's a pleasure," I replied. "Come and sit down. Breakfast isn't ready yet. We have the coffee now, though."

We sat on the old chairs next to the table. There were only enough chairs for the three of us. We were rarely lucky enough to get more than one or two guests at a time. I poured Josiah a cup of coffee and we started to chat.

"Anything interesting been going on lately?" I inquired.

"Nothin' too out of the ordinary. I heard the gunsmith got a shipment of Smith and Wessons in a few days ago. They've been selling like sweet tea in July."

"Well that's fine by me, long as he sells them to more Sheriffs than outlaws," I snickered to myself.

Maddy brought out the coffee and filled our metal cups to the brim.

"Thank you, ma'am," said Josiah. He took a sip.

"How's the bank been? Has business been good?" I asked.

"Well, I would say it's going about as well as I can expect. A bank is going just fine, unless it's getting robbed, if you ask me. Still, people ain't visiting the bank as much as I'd like. It seems these days the only people that show up are withdrawing money for camp supplies," Josiah laughed. There was a pause for a second.

"Why would so many people want camp supplies right now?" I asked. Something about his statement sounded a bit suspicious.

"Well…" said Josiah, thinking. "I hear they're out huntin' for Patsy Harriot's necklace. It's an old myth from around here. I'm sure the necklace ain't around here, though. If it had been, someone would have found it years ago."

I pondered this for a moment. It sounded intriguing. Now, I wanted to know more about the old legend.

"Josiah, can you tell me that story, please?" I asked.

"I suppose I could. It's been told a million times, but there wouldn't be no difference telling it again," Josiah laughed a little more, and spilled a few drops of coffee from the cup he was holding. As he talked, he sipped his drink.

"It started when Patsy Harriot moved into Raton in 1870. She was one of the richest girls in Texas at the time. Her father had been murdered by William Thompson's grandpa, Paul Thompson. She saw him get killed herself. Patsy got so hateful of Paul Thompson that she followed him all the way over to this area in New Mexico Territory. A brave, brave soul for a girl of age 14. Now, Paul Thompson was a stone-cold killer. The legend says that he finally captured her, dropped her into an underground cave, and left her for dead. Dropped her 6 feet under the ground, fully alive, and secured it with a boulder on top. Didn't have the decency to just shoot the girl. Poor young girl suffered there for days or maybe weeks; finally died of thirst, famine, exhaustion, or maybe plain ol' insanity. And the legend has it that if you stand by the cave, you can hear the girl's bloodcurdling wails, even to this day…" he paused. I suddenly became aware of shivers on my arms.

He continued. "Patsy adored her daddy. He was her hero. On her tenth birthday he had given her a nice, purty necklace… After he died, Patsy never took off that necklace. She wore it day and night. I guess it was her last connection to her daddy after he died…When Paul Thompson was on his deathbed a while later, he mentioned that he never took off that necklace from Patsy Harriot when he dropped her in the cave. That probably means it's still buried somewhere in that cave. The reason why people are so excited about this is that her necklace was made of pure gold with a diamond and rubies in the center. They say it's as shiny as a new Double Eagle. There's a nice lil' cross on it, too. I think Patsy herself was a Methodist. Anyways, it's a pretty darned expensive piece of jewelry. People would pay a fortune for it, especially considering the story of what happened to it. Today, and because of the legend behind it—that piece is worth a fortune."

Josiah stared at his empty coffee cup. He had taken sips throughout the story, until he was done with his drink. I waited in anticipation for the rest of the story.

"Now, I am not completely sure why all these people are headed to look for the necklace all of a sudden. It may be that the Albuquerque Journal finally printed an article about the necklace. Or maybe the word of mouth finally got around. I'm not sure… I do hear that Thompson Gang is out lookin' though. They ain't nothin' but darned trouble. I hope they move back to Colorado where they belong." Josiah paused.

"I don't like them people." I said. "They killed my grandfather. Bill Thompson himself did, actually. I guess I have a score to settle with him."

Josiah shook his head, empathizing with my dislike of the Thompson Gang. Maddy suddenly walked in with a few plates worth of steaming sausage, biscuits, and fried eggs. I stood up quickly. Josiah continued to spew.

"The Thompson Gang has been causing trouble and raisin' Cain on this area for years… what I would do to get my hands on them myself… I ain't no gunslinger, but I wish I were now, since they're around. Really, Bill Thompson himself is the leader, and nothin' would really go well without him. He's smart and lucky. He ain't never got shot. And the rest of the group are his followers. But I have a feeling if you were to get rid of him – the rest would go with him somehow or other. Straight to hell."

"Excuse me for a second." I heard Maddy coming, and I wanted to protect her from this conversation. She was a sensitive woman, and didn't deserve to hear so much talk of hatred and murder. Even though I wanted to talk more with Josiah, I would have to wait a while. I met Maddy at the doorsill and led her to the table. She then poured us each another cup of steamy coffee.

"How have you been, Mister Tucker?" asked Maddy.

"Purty good. How about you?" said Josiah.

Their conversation skipped over my head like a rock over water. I thought about what Josiah had told me, and about that secret passageway I had discovered the night before. Could I have actually been in the location of Patsy Harriot's treasure? I felt regretful that I had never opened up the door to the cave completely. There was a good chance I would never be able to find the place again. My thoughts turned to my horse, which often seemed to cause trouble like he did at the cave. Damn! I may have been so close to stumbling on that necklace!   "Darn horse," I muttered under my breath.

The meal went by with regular conversation, but nothing that had to do with the treasure or the Thompson Gang. After breakfast, the three of us went out on the porch to relax and stare at the desert for a few minutes. We didn't talk much. I looked out at all the heat rising like smoke from a barbeque. I went into a bit of a trance, staring ahead of me. It was smothering hot, even in the shade. I felt lethargic and unable to move for a while. My mind was still pondering t the legend, the cave, the necklace.

Once a good chunk of time had passed, I said goodbye to Josiah. He hopped on his horse and rode off onto the trail. I stayed on the chair and thought more about the treasure. Should I take the risk and try to seek the treasure? Or was I just dreaming? Who knew what could be in store for me if I found that legendary old necklace. It could be the start of a whole new life for Maddy and I. These past years had been grueling, trying to survive in the heartless West. I wanted to protect her, and offer her a life fit for royalty Or at least fit for a country girl with a heart of gold.

At four o'clock that day, I made up my mind to head out and try to find Patsy Harriot's necklace. The way I saw it, there wasn't too much I could lose, as long as I didn't get myself lost or shot.

"Maddy, I am going to Mr. Charleston's ranch to see if he has a job for me…." I said. I regretted making up the white lie about Mr. Charleston, but I needed to have some excuse to go out and look for treasure like a fool.

I walked in my room and pulled out my old riding chaps and spurs. As I was about to head out, I saw our old Colt revolver on top of my dresser. I wasn't very interested in guns, but I knew the Thompson Gang was also out there, looking for the same treasure. I decided to pack iron just in case. I had only carried a gun once before; on the trip down to New Mexico.

Taking the revolver off the dresser, I examined it. It wasn't loaded, since Maddy thought loading it would cause more harm than good. I let her win that argument. Still, an unloaded gun would be useless if I encountered a serious outlaw posse like the Thompson Gang. I winced at the thought of actually shooting someone. I wasn't born out West, and since Kansas was settled, I'd never seen anyone get shot first-hand.

I'd bought the used revolver a few days after moving to New Mexico. I remembered the few times I went shooting with my dad. He'd taught me the basics, but I had doubts about the basics being enough in a real fight.

I could draw and shoot accurately enough, but I knew a lot of cowboys could shoot from the hip faster than greased lightning.

I studied the old gun. It was silver plated, but the silver was starting to wear off. There were small patches of rust on it as well. The internal parts worked, but weren't very smooth. I holstered the revolver and dug around in the drawers until I found a box of Remington pistol cartridges. I put a few in my pocket.

Trying to remember how to load the revolver was difficult. I cocked the hammer until it clicked three times, and tried to open the loading gate, but it wouldn't open. Frustrated, I pulled the trigger, let the hammer down, and cocked the hammer again. This time, I only made it click once. I opened the loading gate and sluggishly placed five cartridges inside the revolver.

I remembered my father telling me to only load five cartridges and put the hammer where the sixth should be. He told me this because if the hammer touched the sixth cartridge, you could shoot your foot or leg if the hammer got struck by something.

I put the revolver in the holster and went outside, feeling very authoritative. Since I rarely wore a gun, it made me feel all the more powerful when I did. William was out in the pasture. He looked up at me for a second, then put his head down and continued to eat hay. I took the rope off the fence and entered the pasture. I grabbed a handful of hay and asked William to come over. He considered my offer for a second, and then walked towards me. I slipped the rope around his neck and walked him towards the gate entrance. Then, I saddled William up and walked him back towards the house to say goodbye to Maddy one last time.

"I'll see you later, Maddy. I love you." I tipped my hat to my wife. She waved as I trotted away.

15

Of course, William was hardly contented with a trot. He snorted and put his ears back. He wanted to go a little faster. I stood up a little in the saddle and slapped William on the neck. He burst into a blistering gallop. If there was anything good about William, it was that he could really run if necessary.

Ironically enough, I tired before William did. Although I was fit enough to ride, I wasn't used to a sustained gallop. As I slowed William back down into a fast trot, I could tell he was a little disappointed.

I kept on the trail that ran perpendicular to the house. I started to see, way off in the distance, some of the rock formations I had ridden past the night before. My heart raced a little faster. For some reason, my stomach churned a little bit. I really felt I knew the location of the necklace.

As I rode on towards the rock formations, I felt some apprehension about trying to find the necklace. Maybe it was because Josiah had mentioned the Thompson Gang out there. It could also be because my horse seemed so afraid of the area.

I didn't listen to my racing heart, or my churning stomach, though. I rode on until I reached a rock formation. William slowly walked around the formation, but neither of us found the entrance to the cave. I sighed. There were so many other rock formations in the area. Although I had a general idea of where the cave was, my memory of the last night wasn't perfect. I wished I had drunk a little less whiskey.

Tired out from the long ride, I dismounted and put William's reins on the ground. I snickered a bit, knowing he would trip on the reins if he tried to escape. In front of me was a rock about the perfect size to sit on. I stood beside it for a few minutes, until my shadow cooled the rock down enough to sit on.

I took a canteen off my side and drank some. William stared at me curiously. He sniffed the canteen.

"Okay, boy. You can have some water, too."

I poured some water in my fry pan. Since he sweated so much from the gallop, William absorbed the water like a sponge. He happily slurped up three fry pans full, and I could tell he wanted even more.

I laid down on the rock for a while. Although I had slept in more comfortable beds before, this one would do for a while. I slowly but surely fell asleep.

It was about six o'clock when I woke up. My horse was standing there with his eyes shut. He had fallen asleep when I did. I snapped my fingers, and Williams eyes flew open. I yawned, and got up. I rode out to the next rock structure. It wasn't the right one, either. As I started to walk away from the next formation, I spotted someone's camp a few minutes away. Although I didn't realize it, I rode on a little closer to the camp as I traveled to the next rock structure. There were at least three men at the camp, but there could have been more. I vaguely wanted to see what they were up to and maybe stay there for the night, but I avoided the camp.

By the time I nearly reached the next possible treasure spot, my horse was getting tired, and so was I. I fed him a molasses oat treat, and gave him some more water. He was a little happier after that. The sun was getting low in the sky, and I knew I had to hurry, or else I would have to go home empty-handed. I vowed that if this rock formation wasn't the right one, I would quit looking for the necklace. I walked towards the rock. I started to breathe a little faster when I saw that strange brown rock where the orange rock should be. It was the right place. I ran towards the cave entrance.

"Stay right here, mister. I don't need you spooking again!" I said to William.

I pushed at the rock with all of my might. It slowly slid to the side. After about ten seconds, I had just enough room to sneak into the cave. I lit a match to illuminate the inside.

Walking through the narrow passage, I was scared. There could be just about anything inside, including bandits who preyed on people like me. I could only see a few feet ahead of me.

Suddenly, I saw a skeleton on the ground in front of me. It was right at the end of the passageway. A chill went down my spine. I slowly moved towards it. The body was wearing the thin remains of woman's clothing, so I assumed it was Patsy Harriot.

I carefully examined the floor around Patsy Harriot's corpse, but there was nothing interesting there. Then, I held my breath and tried to find the necklace on the body itself.

Nothing.

My eyes widened, and my blood started to rush. I walked over to the wall and kicked it. I had been sure I was in the right spot. It looked the same. The only solution was that the necklace was gone or had never even been in the cave to begin with. Or, someone else had already discovered it.

I wasn't going to look too closely, or I could risk getting bit by a snake or stung by a scorpion hiding on the rotted body. I knew the necklace wasn't on Patsy's neck, and it wasn't bulging in her pocket, either. I grunted. Someone had probably taken the necklace a long time ago. Either that or maybe it never even existed in the first place.

As I started to walk out of the cave, I became very tense and rushed. I really needed to escape that creepy room at the end of the passage. How had she died in the first place? I hurried as fast as I could go without the match burning out. I saw some light at the end of the passageway. William nickered. Had I spooked him, or was it someone else?

I ran out of the cave. Right beside me, a foot away, was a rough old man. He had a colt pistol pointed right at my head. My heart stopped.

"Give me the necklace!," he roared.
My eyes blurred for a second. I had no idea what to say.
"Okay, just give me a second," I replied. My heart raced faster than it ever had before. I could hardly think. I unconsciously moved my hand closer to my revolver.
"I ain't givin' you a damned second! Give me the jewelry or I'll give you a bullet right in your head!" snapped the man.
I drew my pistol and pulled the trigger. BANG! The outlaw reeled backwards from the force.
"Damn!" he yelled, falling to the ground. He struggled, dropped his gun, and rolled around on the ground. He was bleeding severely.

I panicked and ran away from the rock. I saw that my horse had spooked, and I could see him a while away, still running from the sound of the gunshot.

I hoped the camp I had seen earlier didn't care about what had just happened. If they did, I could be in even more trouble. I kept running after my horse, panicking more about the fact that I had just shot a man.

My horse stopped running, and I hopped on him. As soon as I got on William, I kicked him hard. He took off as fast as he could. Horses can read your mind; if you need them to go fast, they will.

My worst nightmare became true. Off in the distance, I saw the campers saddle up and start to chase after me. They must have all been in the Thompson Gang, along with the man who tried to rob me. I was, however, fortunate that they didn't all rob me at the same time.

The outlaws galloped towards me, but they couldn't gain much ground against my young Quarter Horse. I heard a shot or two hit the ground about ten yards away from me, which only spooked my horse more.

The trail to my house was in sight, only seconds away. If I could get on the trail, there would be a good chance the outlaws would stop chasing me.

William ran and ran until he got us to the trail. I took another look back at the outlaw posse. They were not too far away, but I was confident I could beat them.

I kicked my horse back into a gallop, and headed back towards the house. Since I knew the lay of the land, I devised a plan to lose the outlaws. I veered my gelding into a piece of land off the path with a lot of rocks. In the growing darkness, I doubted the outlaws could tell the difference between me and the rocks. To be extra careful, I dismounted after I had passed the rocks.

BANG! I heard gunshots and shouting. One of the outlaws shot a rock only twenty yards in front of me. I heard pieces of it hit the ground nearby. My horse became scared and threw his head up high. I tried to calm him down.

I drew my pistol and tried my best to aim it at the only outlaw I could see. BANG! BANG! BANG! I fired three times to be sure I didn't miss. At the second shot, the man fell off his horse and the other men fled. I hopped on William and rode away from the scene as fast as lightning, leaving a lifeless body behind me.

CHAPTER 3
Raton, New Mexico, June 25, 1897:

After a few more tense minutes of riding, I returned home. My wife greeted me at the door. Her face was worried.

"I thought you'd be back earlier. How was it over at Mister Charleston's ranch? Did he have a job for you?" asked Maddy.
"No. He says he's got as many hands as he has room for… I'm really tired," I replied, trying to dodge the question as much as possible.
"Why are you carryin' a gun? Do you have a problem with someone?"
"I just felt like I should carry it today. Just a hunch. Besides, this town ain't old enough to be safe yet," I said.
"Don't tell me you wore that gun into town. They don't allow pistols. Come to speak of it, I did hear some gunshots, recently. Some of them sounded like they were really close, too! Do you know what happened? I hope it wasn't one of those Gang posses," inquired Maddy.
"Don't worry. I didn't wear it into town. I don't know. It might have been the Thompson Gang," I said blankly. I disliked lying, but I feared telling the truth.
Standing there for a few seconds, I felt very awkward.
"I am going to bed. Goodnight!" I said hastily.
"You never go to bed this early," replied Maddy, her brow furrowed with concern.
"I know. I just feel really tired tonight. I've been riding a lot."
"Goodnight then," replied Maddy, walking into the kitchen.

I walked over to the bedroom and lay down. I tried my best to fall asleep, but my mind kept spinning and churning. It seemed like I would never fall asleep. Images of the day raced through my head. I still heard the outlaw's voice, rough as sandpaper, as he tried to take the non-existent necklace from me. I started to wonder why I had even tried to find the necklace in the first place. It's not like I seriously thought it was anything but a myth, anyways.

I laid there until my wife had long since fallen asleep, and she went to bed later than I did. However, all the energy I had expended running away from the bandits had made me exhausted. Although my mind kept racing and refusing to fall asleep, I had to get my energy back from all the riding.

Eventually, I fell into a light sleep filled with nightmares and bizarre dreams. My mind was scarred by the events of the day.

Waking up soaked with sweat, I tried to remember what had happened. The sunlight shone through the windows, so I knew it was morning. "Get up, Clint," said my wife. She was standing in the doorway, looking like she had been up for a while. I'd slept in.

It took me much longer to get up than usual. I had to walk over to the well to wash my face, and revive myself a bit. I wondered if I should pack the revolver in the house, just in case. It might scare Maddy, but I felt I needed to. I finally decided to un-tuck my shirt and carry it between my belt and my pants.

I was supposed to head off into town and help a friend with his job there that morning. We ate a quick and simple breakfast, and I tried my best to sound normal to Maddy. She seemed to think I was in a strange mood, though, despite all my efforts to appear normal.
"I have to go help Buntam Harvert with the saloon renovation. I should be done before sundown," I said to Maddy.
"Good luck with that. I hope you work like you actually do renovations," Maddy joked.
"Yep. I'll try my best," I replied, trying to be funny but falling flat again. Saddling up William, I noticed he was still a bit tense and nervous from the day before. His tail twitched repeatedly, and he often put his ears back when I tried to talk to him. He was also quite lame from the extended gallop over rough terrain. One of his legs dragged behind him slightly, which I knew would be a problem on the ride out to town. I

guessed the injury wasn't permanent, but I wasn't sure. I inspected the sore leg closer, and decided it wasn't bad enough to last very long.

I went inside, and asked Maddy if I could ride her horse, Betty. She seemed a little suspicious about William being lame, but told me I could take Betty anyways.

Betty was a ten year old paint horse. She was even-tempered, and less given to spooking than William. However, she didn't have the speed or stamina of William.

I hopped on Betty, and trotted her off our property. I sincerely hoped the outlaw band wasn't still looking for me. There was only a small chance I could get away or shoot them if I encountered them again.

Betty breezed along the path at a respectable, but modest pace. We kept on the path for around ten minutes at that speed.

A few boulders came up beside the path. I did not really pay much attention to it until it was only thirty feet in front of us.

Suddenly, a group of three men leaped out from the rock. I recognized them as the men who I'd seen in the camp when I was looking for the necklace. I gasped and reined my horse, frozen.

"We know who you are, you worthless thumb-suckin' horse-stealin' man-killin' varmint! I know you killed James Whitney! We was good friends. I didn't want him to die. So I am gonna hang you like the cow pile you are. Ain't nobody wrongs Bill Thompson or none of his friends and gets through it alive!" shouted the leader of the gang. He was a filthy mess, dirt buried in the wrinkles and scars of his face. I was sure he hadn't been in a town or a bathtub in weeks.

The outlaws had two pistols and a rifle pointed right at my head. I started to panic. With my gun under my shirt, I knew it would take far too long to draw and fire. There wasn't much I could do. If I tried to run away, either I or my horse would surely be shot. I kept my hands away from the gun, so I wouldn't get shot for looking like I was about to draw.

"What do y'all want from me? I'm only carrying twenty cents into town." The leader laughed and spit some tobacco juice on the ground. He angrily smothered it with his boot.

"Dammit all, I already told you that we don't want yer' stinkin' money. I want more than that! I want yer' lifeless body hangin' from a tree. Your money would be nice, too. But I'll be sure to take it out of yer' pocket when you're dead."

Bill Thompson snorted, laughed, looked at one of his friends, and nodded.

"You can either try to run and get shot, or you can get off that horse right now!" threatened Bill Thompson.

I thought about my options for a few seconds. I could never get away from the outlaws. I was better off trying to escape later than getting shot right then. I could only hope I could get a chance to get away from them or get my gun before they killed me.

I dismounted and stood next to my horse. One of Bill's fellow outlaws walked up to me and tied my hands and legs up roughly. I started to panic. I had no conceivable way to get out of the mess I was in. I could hardly shoot to save my life, and my horse wouldn't help me. Bill's helper threw me up on his horse and mounted it. I felt very awkward and helpless.

"Now, we just gotta find a tree!" said Bill Thompson. My mind was stuck on one thought.

Oh my God, I'm gonna die!

That thought played like a broken phonograph record as we rode away towards the wilderness. Out of the corner of my eye, I could see a man and his horse running towards the town.

Damn coward. I thought to myself. *He could at least come over here and see what's happening to me. That's what I would do if I were him!*

I kept bumping along on that horse for a god-awful long time. I would often hit my nose on the saddle bag, or land on some sharp part of the saddle. I didn't know whether I wanted to be hung right at that moment or long afterwards.

Dear Jesus, please save me! Or at least take me to Heaven darned quick!
Luckily, there was not an abundance of trees in New Mexico. It would take them at least ten minutes to find a suitable tree.

"I can't find no trees," said Bill Thompson. "Why don't we just shoot him?"
"I ain't too sure. People could hear it and find the body."
My blood ran cold. I felt faint. I tried to struggle, and get untied, but it was useless.
"I donno. Who's the boss around here, anyways?" replied Bill, getting angry.
"Ok! Shoot him if you want to!"
"Gosh darn it!" I yelled, losing my temper and my mind. "Y'all are gonna' pay for this! You can't get away with hanging a person who was just using self-defense! I didn't know that man was one of your posse!"
"Shut up!" replied Bill. "He was, and I'll bet you knew that and killed him for no damn reason." He walked over to me with his revolver. I held my breath and prayed that I wouldn't get shot. Bill slammed me with the butt of his revolver.
"Owww!" I yelled. A horrible burning pain engulfed my leg. My vision went blurry. I stopped talking.

"Hey, Bill!" yelled one of Bill's partners. "I found a tree!"
"Hell, I was just about to shoot the varmint. But I guess we're better off hangin' him if it's quieter."

The horse I was on was led in-hand over to the tree. Even though I had gone through tense moments in my life before, this was by far the worst. I was terrified. The man who had tied me up took a long rope from his saddle. I could see him try to tie it into a noose, out of the corner of my eye. He seemed to be struggling. I chuckled to myself.

"Darned rope!" said the man. He fumbled around with it more until the rope was made into a big knot.
"Dammit!" he yelled. Bill walked over and forcefully grabbed the rope from the other man.
"You good-for-nothing jerk!" he yelled. "Why are you even in this posse if you can't tie a noose? You are a useless piece of second-rate half-breed garbage."
"I'm sorry, Bill!"

Bill spat more tobacco juice on the ground. He tried his best to untie the knot, but it was pretty tangled up. He grunted in frustration. I didn't feel like laughing any more. It would only be a matter of seconds before Bill would tie the rope up right.

"Ha! Got it. Now, you are gonna HANG!" hissed Bill, his snakelike face thrust right in front of me. Bill took the noose and put it around my neck. He tightened it until I could hardly breathe, letting out sinister fits of laughter.
"Who's laughin' now, huh? Not you! Larry, throw the other half of this rope over that tree branch and tie it to your horse."
Larry did as was instructed. I didn't hardly feel anything in my body. It was like I was already numb. It felt like a dream.

"Okay. It's tied to the saddle."
"Good," replied Bill. "You know what to do."

I held my breath. Larry took a rein in his hand. He raised it up, about to smack his horse with it. My eyes were frozen open.

BANG! I felt a strange release of tension on my neck. I fell to the ground. I rolled over.

What the hell just happened? Then, I realized it. I wasn't hanging, I was on the ground. Someone had shot the rope. Half of it dangled from the tree, the other half was still tethered to my neck. I looked off in the distance, towards the trail. I could see a United States Marshal, two hundred yards away, his rifle letting out a gentle puff of smoke.

"God damn it!" screamed Bill, realizing what had happened. The outlaws forgot about hanging me, and drew their revolvers. They started to fire, but their aim wasn't as good as the Marshal's, since he'd had the drop on them, and was armed with a large rifle. I saw Larry drop to the ground, along with another man whom I didn't know the name of. They screamed in pain.

Outnumbered by the Marshal and his deputy, Bill Thompson mounted his own horse and rode off. He moved faster than a Thoroughbred at the start of a race. The horse that used to be attached to my rope had run off from the gunfire. I didn't see Betty anywhere. I hoped she didn't run off into the wilderness.

Since I was still bound up, I couldn't reach my revolver. I could have assisted the law if I could, though. Either way, two of the outlaws were either dying or injured.

I watched the Marshal and his deputy walk over to me. They severed the rope from my hands and legs. The noose took a while to cut through, but they eventually took that off my neck.

"Thank you so much. I was at death's door for a minute there!" I said, gasping.

"That's what we're here for." replied the Marshal. "Now get on my horse and we'll ride double. Where'd your horse go to?"

"She ran off."

"Well, you better hope she don't get stolen or ate up by some wild animal. Come with me. You have some questions to answer."

"Wait a second, Marshal. How did you get over here? You were just in time! I don't get it."

The Marshal chuckled and smiled. "I just had a hunch somethin' was going on. Couldn't tell just what, but I rode out here and saw you gettin' hung. I'll tell you, it ain't nothin' bad when you listen to them little hunches. I've saved other people like you before."

I was amazed. "Wow. You're a commendable man."

The Marshal didn't reply, but I could see him grinning.

CHAPTER 4
Raton, New Mexico, June 25, 1897:

I was sent to the Marshal's office immediately. It was a small room, with only a few chairs, a desk, and a jail cell. I sat on a stool across from the Marshal's desk. He sat up straight and serious. I found no other alternative than to tell the truth.

"What's your name, Mister?" asked the Marshal.
"Clint Patterson."
"I'm Marshal Lee Johnson." He flashed his star.

Marshal Johnson was a tall man, and quite intimidating to almost anyone he met. He wore an oiled dark brown leather vest, with a star gleaming so bright the entire world could see it. He had a weathered, pitted face and a grey mustache. He packed two Colt Model 3 Schofields, shining like the sun at high noon. He carried the butts facing forward, so he could draw with the hand on the opposite side of the

gun.

I'd heard about the fancy revolvers from one of my friends, but never seen one flashed in public. They were unique and fascinating looking, to say the least.

"So what got you up in that tree?" asked the Marshal.

I hesitated for a second. "Well, it's a long story. I was riding home from town a few days ago, and I came across some strange rock. The next day, I heard from my friend that Patsy Harriot's necklace could be where I went to the night before. I went over there, but I never found the necklace. Instead, I got robbed and chased back to my house. A posse found me the next day and tried to hang me. I would have died if you didn't save me. I owe you my life."

"I know that," replied Marshal Johnson, rather mundanely. I wondered how many lives he had saved during his career.
"Did you kill anyone?" asked the Marshal.
"Yessir," I said, uneasy.
"Who?" asked the Marshal, not particularly interested.
"The man who tried to steal the necklace."
"But you never found the necklace," said the Marshal.
"I know. But he would never have believed me. I had no choice but to shoot him. He drew on me first."
"Sure. You'll get off for that. I really don't care what happened with you, honestly. You ain't no outlaw, and that's all that matters. Hell, I can tell the whole darned thing really messed with your head," Marshal Johnson said, reading me like a book.
"I only have one regret- and that is that we didn't shoot William Thompson while we had the chance. He is a slippery snake. People have been after him for a long time, and he's got a big price on his head. You've seen how immoral he is. That man's as crooked as a dog's hind leg. "

"Yessir. I know what you're sayin'," I replied.

The Marshal moved in a little closer to me.

"So, I know you're purty good with a gun…"

I interrupted, "I'm not that good with a gun, sir. I'm not a shootin' type of man. In fact, this was the first time I actually shot at someone…"

"Yep, but not many can outshoot someone who drew on 'em first. I recognize skill when I see it. I've been trying to track down William Thompson for a long time…" he said, and paused, looking at me with a glint in his eye as bright as his badge. Then he leaned over and said, in a whisper, "How'd you like to help me catch that no-good rascal?"

I paused for a moment. I couldn't believe my ears. Time seemed to stand still. This wasn't what I had anticipated when I moved to New Mexico.

"What would be in it for me?" I asked. If I were gonna put my life on the line, it had to be for a good reason.

"Let me see. I'll offer you a share of the bounty. And you don't even have to be the one to shoot the varmint. If you can just help capture him so I can shoot him, you'll be livin' like a crow in a cornfield for the rest of your life."

My mind spun with thoughts. It was a risky endeavor. This wasn't a decision that concerned me alone. If I were to put my own life at risk, this would deeply affect my Maddy. Yet, if I somehow succeeded in this venture, it would also affect my Maddy. I could shower her in the life she deserved. My mind conjured up visions of steaming, nourishing meals….maybe a bigger farm…some special jewelry for Maddy.

Finally I gave my answer. "That sounds just fine to me," I replied, a sly smile on my face.

Marshal Johnson chuckled. He took a careful glance outside, and then opened his desk drawer. I saw a bottle of whiskey in his hand.

"Mister Patterson, I believe you made the right choice. That man needs killin," Marshal Johnson replied, pouring us both a shot.

"When should we get down to business?" he asked.

"Pretty darned soon," I replied.

"How 'bout tomorrow?" Marshal Johnson inquired.

I nodded, and we tipped back the glasses and downed our shots.

"Do you have any family, Mister Patterson?" asked Marshal Johnson.

"Yes sir. I have a wife, and my grandmother lives in Kansas. My father recently died from liver disease and my mother is back in Kansas." The Marshal nodded his head.

"Now go be a good husband and tell your wife what yer' doing," said Marshal Johnson.

"I have a job to do over at the saloon, first," I replied.

"That's fine, but be back at my office tomorrow morning at nine o'-clock sharp. I ain't waitin' for you."

I helped move furniture out of a room on the top floor of the saloon. After that, we started to tear down the wallpaper and get the paints out. We managed to paint about half of the room. If it had been a normal day, I could have done much more. However, I was not in the mood to work much, considering I almost died hours before. They were going to strip it and replace it with fancier furnishings and wallpaper. When I was finished with my job, I was paid a quarter by the saloon owner.

When I left the saloon, I saw a strange man holding a horse. I walked up to the man. The horse looked a lot like Betty. As I looked closer at her, I noticed all the markings matched up with Betty's.

"Who does this horse belong to? I saw it run into town a few minutes ago," the man inquired.

"It's my wife's horse, if I'm not mistaken," I replied.

"How do I know for sure?"

"Go in the Sheriff's office and ask the Marshal. He knows every horse in this town."

The man didn't really seem to care about confirming the owner; he just wanted to make sure I wasn't a thief.

"Here she is."

"Thank you very much. Where did you find her?"

"She was runnin' towards the town. I didn't see no rider, so I led her over to the town."

I handed the man a few pennies. I was happy Betty hadn't run off in the desert or got in trouble. I jumped on her and headed out of Raton.

The ride back home was uneventful. It was about four in the afternoon when I arrived. I took my time during the ride. I hitched Betty up to the pole next to our little house. Her eyes were sleepy from the trip.

"You ain't like William, are you? He wouldn't be so tired right now," I said to Betty. I patted her on the cheek. She stared ahead, melancholy. I walked up to the front porch and knocked on the door. Maddy walked over from inside and opened the door.

"Hi, Maddy," I said.

"How'd the job go? Is it coming along?" she asked.

"It's going well. We took all the furniture out of that room upstairs. Now we just have to put some in…" I replied. My voice was strained from the rope biting into my neck.

I noticed Maddy's eyes squinting, and her calm demeanor being replaced with a worried one.

"Clint… what's wrong with your neck? It's all red!" she inquired, in a high-pitched voice. I sighed loudly, took a deep breath and prepared to tell her the story.

"Maddy, I'm sorry. I'm real sorry."

"About what?" she asked, very concerned. I was sad I'd lied to her in the past. It had only complicated things much more.

"I didn't tell you the truth about what I did yesterday. I didn't go over to Mister Charleston's ranch. I did something else," I paused and composed myself.

"Two days ago, I found a door to get in this cave. I tried to find it yesterday, because I thought this old treasure was in it. I got into a pretty big brawl with the Thompson Gang. My Lord, I am mad at them. They almost stretched my neck. But Marshal Johnson saved my life. He shot most of them with his rifle, even though their leader Bill Thompson got off unharmed."

Maddy raised her eyebrows, surprised. She opened her mouth and tried to say something, but no words came out.

"I'm sorry for lying, Maddy. I didn't want to worry you," I repeated. I blinked a few times.

Maddy squeezed me tightly. I could see a tear in her eye.

"It's okay," she whispered. "I'm just happy you're alive."

I held her for a long time. I was amazed she'd forgiven me, since I had expected she would be furious.

"You're my favorite person in this whole darned world. You're my girl," I said, quietly. I rubbed her lovingly on the back a few times.

I ended our embrace and took a step backwards, then gathered my composure and continued.

"Marshal Johnson asked me to hunt down the Thompsons with him and a few of his friends." I took a quick look at the ground.

"I need to see that man be brought to justice. I know fightin' ain't really my way, but this is personal. I never wronged the Thompsons. I have to see them pay for what they've done. I can still remember the day that man took my grandpa's life," I said, with a fire in my voice.

"What? You never told me that before," replied Maddy.

"I know. It's a personal memory. Not one I think about much, either. It happened so long ago. Twelve years ago, Bill Thompson was playing poker with my grandpa at the High Horse Saloon in Albuquerque. My grandpa played as fair as a Russian shut-in's skin, but he got in a fight with Bill Thompson over 'cheating.' The two of them had it out in a fistfight, and my grandpa won. Bill wasn't happy about losing. He needed to preserve his reputation, so he murdered my grandpa that night in cold blood."

"That's horrible."

"It is." I shook my head. "I have some business with the Thompsons, and I'm not giving up until every last one of them is in the pen or in Hell. I'll promise you that."

"I won't stop you. But I don't think it's a good idea. It's dangerous looking for a wanted outlaw, and I'm worried about you," said Maddy.

"It is dangerous. I know that. I hope there will be enough of us to be a good match for him. There's always a good chance he has some more friends he'll pick up. We'll have to catch him fast while he's alone."

"I just hope you come home soon," Maddy said, softly. She looked at the ground, melancholy.

"I do too." I replied.

It took a few hours to get my belongings together. I had a lot of gear to stuff in the saddlebags. I packed some food, a cast iron fry pan, my revolver, two canteens, and some rope.

I walked outside and found William, eating hay. I inspected him closely.

"Looks like you ain't so sore anymore," I said, relieved.

William nickered softly. I saddled him up and walked him back to the house.

"You better be a good boy on this trip. If you spook at the wrong moment, I could get in a lot of trouble. Understand me?" I asked. I looked into William's eyes. He looked like he knew what I was talking about.

Maddy opened the door to the house. She saw that I was ready to leave. I walked up to her.

"I love you. I'll be back as soon as I'm done," I said.

"I love you too. Good luck. Get back here as soon as you can. That man deserves some manila fever."

We hugged a final time, and I hopped on William and headed off, back into town. I hoped I would live to see my house and my dear wife again. I took one last look at the cabin and Maddy waving to me, as I took to the main road to Raton. I had no idea what lied ahead, but I knew for sure that no matter what would happen in the end, my whole life was about to change.

CHAPTER 5
Raton, New Mexico, June 25:

I entered the sheriff's office. The Marshal sat at his desk, staring off into space. It took a few seconds for him to notice I was there.

"Now we just have a few more strings to tie up before we leave." explained Marshal Johnson.

"First, let me see that rusty old gun of yours," said the Marshal to me, obviously disapproving of it. I handed the revolver to him. He promptly unloaded it and tossed it in the gun cabinet. I stared at him, wide-eyed. "I'm surprised that darned piece of junk even shot for you! You should remember to never load all six chambers unless you put the hammer in between them and tie it down."

"Marshal!" I said loudly and angrily. "You can't just toss my gun away like a dead rat."

An enigmatic smile broke over the Marshal's face.

"I'm not as wicked a person as you think I am," he said, grinning. I had no idea what he was talking about.

"Follow me for a minute."

"Where?" I asked. He didn't reply.

Promptly, Marshal Johnson escorted me over to a gun shop a few stores down the street. We walked in. The Marshal tipped his hat to the owner.

"How are you, Matt Sundert?"

"Good. And what can I do for you today?" replied the man.

Showing me a cabinet full of pistols, the Marshal spoke to me.

"Take any one of these you want. I didn't throw your gun out for no reason."

"Damn, Marshal, you *are* kind," I said.

I stared for at least five minutes at the beautiful, new firearms. They gleamed like silver. There were so many. Colt Peacemakers, Colt Navies,

Colt Armies, Colt police revolvers, Smith and Wesson double actions, black powder pistols, Remington derringers, and many others filled the cabinet. I had probably never seen so many guns before in my whole life, and definitely never that many in a single store. I realized I had to ask the Marshal for help in choosing a gun.

"Marshal sir, help me decide."
"There's something else here, if you're lookin' for something different," said Joe. There was an air of mystery in his voice.
"It just arrived from Germany. A German man came over to Raton a few months ago, but he got shot. Now we have his gun for sale."
Joe Sundert unlocked a drawer hidden from my sight. He pulled out a cutting-edge technological marvel. It was a C96 Mauser automatic pistol, which looked like it had been made in another world.

The revolver as we know it was invented in 1836. It served throughout the West with authority for seventy years. I got to see with my own eyes what would eventually replace the Colt revolver. I had never seen the likes of it in my entire life. The gun had much more angular, square lines than the elegant revolvers I was so used to. It was made for killing, not target practice, hunting, or anything else American guns excelled at.
"This gun can shoot ten rounds as fast as you can pull the trigger."
"What's the price?" asked the Marshal.
"Two hundred dollars," replied Joe, hardly keeping a straight face.
Marshal Johnson looked at me and shook his head. I knew we could never afford the gun. I was half disappointed and half relieved. I wanted to conservatively stick to a revolver, but I also knew I might not ever see a German pistol again.
Marshal Johnson explained that he would never have enough money for the gun. I didn't, either. Sadly, I ruled out the Mauser.
"Okay. For the pistol, do you want something big or small?" he asked me.
"Something pretty big, but something I can draw quickly," I replied.
"A gun that'll kill in one shot?" asked the Marshal.

"Yes sir."
He chuckled, thought for a minute, and put his hand on his chin. "Give him the five and a half inch barrel Colt Frontier double-action," said the Marshal to the storekeeper.

The man handed a shiny, nickel plated revolver to me. It looked much better than my old gun and had a longer barrel. With it, he gave me two boxes of twenty cartridges.

"Does it work like the other revolver I had?" I asked.
"Purty much. But the front sight's serrated and painted black so it don't reflect the sun so much. And it's a double action, so you don't have to worry about cocking the hammer every shot. It'll work better fer you I'm sure."
"Let's hit the trail." I said to the Marshal, excited to have a new gun.
"What do you mean? You don't even have a rifle! You can't kill outlaws with just a pistol. Maybe John Wesley Hardin could, but not you," explained the Marshal, snickering.

He picked out an equally good-looking rifle for me. It was made out of dark stained walnut and gleaming brass. I shouldered it. The sights lined up naturally and perfectly. It was a fine firearm.

"This ol' Winchester will take the same ammunition as your pistol." He explained. "That way you won't have to carry two cartridge belts. Those forty-four caliber rounds will kill anything up to a bear in a few shots. Those guns might not have the range of my Winchester High-wall, but they work like a charm for close-in fights. Plus my rifle only has the one shot. This 'ere thing can shoot six times in a row."

"Thank you!" I replied. I knew how great the Marshal's rifle was, since he was able to split the rope with it from a considerable distance.

"Have you shot a rifle before?" asked Marshal Johnson.

"Once," I replied.

"Well, we should get some practice in if you really want to take on the Thompson Gang with us."

Marshal Johnson slammed a fifty-dollar bill on the table. Then, me and the Marshal walked out of the store, and tipped our hats to the owner. I was confident we could take on the Thompson Gang.

The two of us rode over to the saloon to meet one of the Marshal's friends. As I hitched my horse up, I spoke with Marshal Johnson.

"Who is this person? Is he helping us find Bill Thompson?"

"I'll tell you when we get inside," replied the Marshal, discreetly.

We walked into the old bar. Sitting on a stool at the counter was a rough-looking middle-aged man. He was dressed in a red plaid shirt and chaps. He was both tall and wide. He probably weighed about two hundred pounds. He had lots of thick long, brown hair. There was some stubble on his tanned face, which had some visible scars. He stared at me suspiciously, like he thought I was a questionable person.

"Mister Bob Peters, meet Mister Clint Patterson," said the Marshal. "Bob Peters will help us track down Bill Thompson and his gang and bring them to justice. He's been in the bounty business for years. Now just so you know, Clint, we're splittin' this bounty money up. You ain't gettin' it all."

"That's fine with me, mister," I replied.

"Nice to meet ya,'" drawled Bob Peters. He extended his hand. We shook. A second later, Bob whispered something in the Marshal's ear. I couldn't make out what it was.

"Patterson, get me a whiskey, please," said the Marshal.

As I bought him a drink, the two men talked. I could faintly make out what they said.

"Darned greenhorn'll get himself killed," whispered Bob.

"I'm not too sure. He can fend for himself. He was outnumbered real bad when I rescued him. He didn't seem too shaken up by it," whispered the Marshal.

"But he'll get in trouble if…" Bob's voice trailed off as the Marshal interrupted him. "Trust me on this one, Bob. This guy's got the skill to kill, he just needs a chance to show it."

Bob fell quiet. I brought the Marshal his drink.

"Thanks for the whiskey." said Marshal Johnson.

I didn't speak much, and neither did the other men. When we noticed we were wasting precious time, we left the saloon. We got on our horses and started off at a quick trot. We went onto a path heading southwest, towards Santa Fe.

During the ride, I got a good look at Bob Peters' horse. He was a very large half-draft horse. I guessed the other half was either Thoroughbred or Warmblood, since the gelding didn't have the pronounced muscles of a Quarter Horse. He looked a lot like Bob Peters himself; big and brawny, with black hair. The horse probably had the same attitude, too.

"Just to make it clear to you, Clint Patterson, I have reasons for tracking down that vermin. He's wanted for horse stealing in Texas, murder in Kansas, murder in New Mexico, and petty crimes just about everywhere. He's been a criminal for longer than the Devil's been evil. The bounty on his head will keep us all high on the hog for a long time," explained Marshal Johnson.

"And I have reasons too," added Bob Peters. "Danged nitwit shot me in the thigh. Darned snake. He deserves a personal beatin' or two. If I could hogtie him up, you should see the things I'd do to that jackass."
"Quiet down," said the Marshal. "We can't bring him in unless he's in decent health, not half-dead. I'll let you get a punch or two in, though. Maybe I'll do the same." Marshal Johnson smiled.
"Darned right you will, Lee," replied Bob Peters, quite imposingly. Marshal Lee Johnson wasn't fazed by the comment, though. He smiled to himself.

We kept going at a trot until seven o'-clock. The sun was sinking lower and bathing the land in a honey-colored light. I could see the rays poking through the mass of clouds. There were some rose clouds interspersed with many grey and blue ones. It was glorious. The sunset was always my favorite time of day, and I found sunsets even more pretty in New Mexico than Kansas.

"Hold up!" shouted Marshal Lee Johnson. We stopped the horses.
"Patterson, see that vulture up there?" he asked.
"Yep, I do."
"Get off your horse and follow me."

I dismounted and followed the Marshal over to a small rock. He kneeled behind it, rifle in hand. Marshal Lee Johnson's rifle was a prestigious and expensive one. The ammunition was three times the price and power of my rifle and revolver ammo. His gun was very large, extremely handsome, and accurate enough to win any target shooting competition.

"Do you know how to shoot a rifle?" asked the Marshal.
"I know the basics. I can hit a milk bottle with one," I replied, timidly.

"Let me see, then. Hit that vulture with my Winchester High-wall."

I stared at the sky. At least a hundred yards away, a huge vulture circled over some carrion. Since the bird was a moving target, it was by no means an easy shot.

I was surprised. I had only shot a rifle a few times before, and never a huge single-shot buffalo rifle like the Marshal's. Marshal Johnson handed the rifle to me. It felt bulky and heavy, with a larger barrel than my brand new Winchesters'.

"Rest the forearm of the rifle on the rock," he instructed. I did as he said.
"Line up the sights, and make sure to aim a little in front of the bird so the bullet can catch up to it. The wind is going towards the right, so aim a few inches to the left."
"Good Lord.," I replied, uneasy.
"Press the trigger real slow-like. Don't move it too quick. It'll jolt the barrel" whispered the Marshal, in anticipation.

I did as he said to the best of my ability. The trigger was so light that it moved quicker than I anticipated. Suddenly, the rifle slammed against my shoulder and made a thunderous BOOM! I saw the shot go a few inches below the bird. The bird's flight was disrupted, but it got its balance back within a second or two.

"Almost," said the Marshal, encouragingly. He took the rifle from me and loaded it again. I took the rifle back and watched the bird. It went in slow, predictable circles. I put the sights right where I supposed the bird would be in a few seconds. I pulled the trigger slowly. BOOM!

I saw a body drop to the ground, followed by dozens of drifting feathers. The vulture was dropped like a slippery dish. I gasped in amazement.

"Damn!" yelled the Marshal. "Not bad!"

"Yee-haw!" shouted Bob Peters. He clapped his hands.

Marshal Lee Johnson rode towards the bird. In a minute, he was back with a large feather. He gave it to me, and I put it in my hatband.

"Looks pretty darned nice," said the Marshal.
We rode on, the Marshal first, me second, and Bob Peters third. Santa Fe was quite a distance away. It would be an overnight ride.

At sunset, we picketed the horses. My horse didn't like Bob Peter's horse. He kept his ears back and kept his distance. I knew they would sort out their differences one way or the other, though.

Marshal Lee gathered some brush and wood for the campfire. Bob Peters leaned on his horse and smoked a cigar. I sat on the ground and thought about where Bill Thompson could be.

The Marshal came back to the fire, and had it roaring within five minutes. We shared a can of beans with some beef jerky strips on the side. I kneeled on my bedroll, and started to talk with the two men.

"Where do you come from, Bob?" I asked.
"I was born in northern Texas. Moved over here 'round ninety-four. I've been around more places than you can count."
"Do you have a family?"
"No sir. Ain't got none. I used to be married, but I ain't anymore. How 'bout you?"
"I have a wife but no kids yet. My dad went up to Heaven a few months ago. He gave me his house. My mother is in Kansas. That's where I was born. I still miss it."
"And I still miss Texas," added Bob, solemnly.
"William Thompson killed my grandpa. Honestly, that's what's fueling this whole manhunt for me."
"How about you, Marshal Johnson?" I asked.

"I've been married for twenty and three years. My wife said she don' want me bounty huntin' no more. I told her this'll be the last time. But I ain't meanin' to retire just yet. I think I may stay around in Raton or even move to Santa Fe."

"What sort of chances do you think we have on this trip?" I asked, regretting the question almost immediately.

"I ain't sure, to be honest. I may just be able to pick him off, but things might not go so well. If they see us too quickly, we'll get in a big ol' gunfight. I hope you'll do well, Mister Patterson."

I kept an awkward silence.

"Hey Bob, I know you're a bounty hunter. How long have you been doing that for?" I inquired, changing the subject.

"I've been bounty huntin' ever since I ran into Bill Thompson," replied Bob. "I've been on his trail for a long time, but I ain't never got closer to him than Mexicans are to Canada, until now. Yes sir. I've been waitin' for darned ever. He's real smart. Maybe he even got a law degree. I can't see a normal person knowing so much about avoidin' the law. He probably learned a thing or two from the inside. But I nabbed a lot of other outlaws. Jason LeRoy, Darrel Wishburn, and Jesse Bayfield are just a few of 'em. I consider it a good living."

"I suppose. But there's some more honest jobs than bounty huntin'. Not like I'm tellin' you how to live your life. It just seems a little… gruesome," I said.

"Watch your mouth, Mister. You ain't doin' nothin' but bounty hunting anyways. I ain't no worse than you are. Besides, I hear all you do is fix stuff. That don' matter compared to keepin' people safe like me. I'll bet I saved a dozen lives by shootin' them outlaws."

I shook my head.

"Y'all keep it calm. I don' need no fight," said the Marshal. I kept my thoughts in check for a moment.

"Well, I guess it's personal. We both hate Bill Thompson. I guess we got some common blood between us, after all. I just mean I wouldn't bounty hunt for a living like you do."

"That's fine with me," snapped Bob Peters. He didn't like long conversations, though, so he stopped talking. I talked for a while with Marshal Lee. After that, I cleaned off my fry pan and extended my bedroll. I ran a rope around my bedroll to try to discourage the snakes. I kept my gun by my side. Getting to know my acquaintances a little more was nice. I already felt more comfortable around them. As I drifted off to sleep, I thought about our cabin. I hoped my wife was doing well without me.

The next morning, we rode off as the sun rose. Santa Fe was only a few hours away. However, the ride passed quite slowly. I contemplated why I was pursuing Bill Thompson in the first place. Of course I was furious at him for tying my noose. He had killed enough people to deserve being killed himself. But there were other reasons as well. Maddy and I were trying our best to get by, but it was much harder to survive in New Mexico than old Kansas. The bounty money would help us survive and maybe even buy a larger house or more land. I hoped my companions would be fair and give me my portion of the reward. A chill went down by back as I considered the very large chance of never getting the money, or even worse, never coming back home.

Marshal Johnson and Bob Peters had talked so much the night before that they were tired of talking, so they rode on silently. Bob Peters only started conversing once the town came up on the horizon, ten miles away. Even from a distance, it sprawled out excessively.

It became hotter and hotter, until my horse was having a hard time trotting so quickly. Sweat rolled down my back. Just as I was about to tell my companions to slow down, I noticed the city in the distance. Compared to the small town of Raton, Santa Fe was massive. However, it was not growing any more. The Western railroad avoided the city for a small town southward, which harmed Santa Fe's economy. Many people had moved away from the city. It seemed like the perfect stop for William Thompson to make on his loop back up to Colorado.

CHAPTER 6
Santa Fe, New Mexico, June 26, 1897:

The Marshal had witnessed Bill Thompson head towards the trail to Santa Fe when he escaped from the scene of the hanging. He had asked some people in Raton if Bill Thompson had entered the town, but no one had seen him. That eliminated the other options. Either Thompson had entered Santa Fe, or bypassed it to go to a town more southward. There was still a good chance of finding out where he went though. Unless he was travelling all the way into Mexico, the Marshal would have the jurisdiction to capture or kill him.

"If Bill Thompson did not go into Santa Fe, he may have traveled directly southward to Las Vegas," explained Marshal Johnson. "He also might have gone up North from here into Espanola on his way back to Colorado."

"I'll bet you he stocked up here for the trip to Espanola. Probably went to the saloon and patronized the girls and the gambling tables there, too. I would if I were him," added Bob Peters, chuckling.

"Do y'all think he would be headed back to Colorado so soon? I thought the Thompson Gang stayed out of their state for longer than that."

"Did you forget that I killed some of his buddies? He's probably going back to Colorado to recruit some more bandits."

"He wouldn't need t' be in Colorado fer' that. There's more outlaws in Sanna' Fe than you kin' shake a stick at," Bob replied.

"I agree. But where would he go if he wasn't headed back to Colorado?" I asked.

The Marshal was visibly confounded. He shook his head.

"We'll have to see what goes on here. I'm sure someone will tell us where he went to. Might take a few dollars, but we'll learn. There's a chance he's galloping down to Mexico right now. He ain't never been there before, but there's always a chance that could happen. Things change, even for outlaws."

We rode into Santa Fe at noon. It was quite possible to lose each other in the stream of people, so we stayed in a rigid single-file line. We found some activities to while away the time. We stopped by the general store to buy some supplies and food. There were a number of restaurants in the town. Bob Peters complained about being hungry, so we headed off to a eatery, hoping to find some edible or maybe even tasty food. The locals thought of us as strange, but weren't hostile like the people from Raton. The restaurant was nothing fancy, and there were only a few unbroken chairs in it. Still, it was better than eating more beans and beef jerky.

We ordered the special for the day, which was some corn mixed with hot Chile pepper, baked beans and coffee. I was hungry from the ride, and thirsty from the scorching desert sun.

I saw a shifty pair of eyes in the corner of the restaurant. I studied the man for as long as I could without him noticing. He was dressed in black, with a large-brimmed hat covering a large portion of his face. He was probably not Bill Thompson, but he still looked suspicious to me. I tried to observe what Marshal Johnson thought of him. His face didn't show much emotion.

The three of us sat down for a second, deciding what to eat. Once the waitress came over, I ordered some cornbread and soup. We chatted until the food arrived.

"Do you have any friends here who might know where the man is?" I asked. The Marshal replied. "I do. Let me think for a second… Bobby Mcdonald might know… I remember! A girl named Catherine James used to be rather… tied up with the guy we're looking for." Marshal Johnson avoided using Bill Thompson's name aloud, possibly because of the suspicious man twenty feet from us.

48

"They were romantic for a while in the past. He might have paid her a quick visit if he went into Santa Fe."

"Who is that?" I whispered, looking over at the suspicious man in black. Although the Marshal shrugged his shoulders, unsure, Bob Peters knew who he was.

"He's Elijah Denton. Used to be in our quarry's little posse. He left and tried to settle down here and make peace with the law. Bet he thinks we're lookin' for him 'stead of Bill Thompson." As usual, Bob let out a raucous laugh.

Our food arrived. As I tried it, I was pleasantly surprised by the quality of Santa Fe food. The food supply in Raton, on the other hand, was extremely boring. Schwede's saloon had never changed its menu, and the general store hardly ever got new groceries in. Santa Fe food tasted fresher, probably because of its proximity to the railroad, which ran twenty miles southward.

We finished our meal in half an hour, taking our time. All of us tried our best to eavesdrop on conversations, and if we were lucky, overhear where Bill Thompson was going off to next. We didn't hear anything particularly unusual, though.

We split up for a few hours, deciding to meet at the saloon later. Unlike the saloon in Raton, the Santa Fe saloon was a hotbed for gambling. I'd overheard someone say it had blackjack, poker, and faro. I was real excited to visit the place.

I explored the town for most of the afternoon. The dusty streets stretched on and on. As I rode, I noticed a Wells Fargo stagecoach unloading money to a bank. I held my breath.

"Whoa," I told William.

I stayed and waited on the opposite side of the road and waited until the deliveryman entered the bank, carrying a large sum of money. A man riding shotgun watched everyone closely. It didn't seem like anyone was going to steal the money. After a tense minute, I rode on.

After a few hours, I headed back to the saloon and waited for my companions. I leaned on the wall and watched people pass by. After about a half an hour, Marshal Johnson returned.

"Where's Bob?" I asked.
"I ain't too sure. You could try to find him. I'll go in the saloon and tell y'all if I see anything interesting."
"Yes, sir," I replied. "Do you have a guess of where he is?"

The Marshal shook his head and entered the saloon. I thought about where Bob Peters could be. He probably wouldn't be riding on the street. I believed he would be inside some building.

I looked around in the bank and the barber, but he wasn't there. Then, I walked back into the restaurant we had eaten at earlier. Not surprisingly, Bob was eating like a hog. He was so busy eating that he didn't even see me until I had stood in front of him for quite a while.

"Hey, Bob. Get yourself in that saloon. We're late," I said.

Bob looked up at me, his mouth full of food. He grimaced.

"Get outta here," he replied after about ten seconds. "I'll be there when I'm done."
I waited for a few more seconds to see if Bob changed his mind. He acted like I wasn't there. I left the restaurant, spiteful. However, I was not about to fight with a hardened bounty hunter. Bob showed up at the Tin Star saloon ten minutes later. We walked in, and shortly found Marshal Johnson sitting at the bar. He was talking to a man sitting next to him whom he seemed to know. There was a shot of tequila on the table in front of him.

"What's goin' on?" asked Bob.

"That man Elijah Denton is in here. I heard Catherine James has a house a few miles from here. There's a chance she knows where Bill Thompson went off too. That is, if he even talked to her. I'm not sure if he remembers that they were together."

"I suppose that's good news. I guess we might as well have some fun here while we have the chance." I replied.

"Darned right," agreed Bob.

"Sorry. I'm a Marshal, and I ain't supposed to gamble. I'll have a drink, though, and try and figure out where our man ran off to. I'm sure someone in here knows."

Bob and I walked away from the bar. He went to the poker table, and I to the blackjack table. There were three other men at the table. Luckily, Elijah Denton was not one of them. I bought twenty-five cents worth of chips.

We were dealt our cards. The dealer's card was an eight. I had a five and a three.

"Hit me," I said.

I received a nine. I now had a seventeen. The other players made their moves, some asking for a hit, and others standing. The dealer flipped his down card over. It was a king, bringing his total up to eighteen. I lost my wager.

"Dang it," I said under my breath.

We played ten more hands until I got tired of blackjack. When I exchanged what used to be a quarter dollar worth of chips, I only got five cents back. My luck was not good.

At least nobody will think I'm cheating. But I'd better play something else, I thought.

51

I stood around for a few minutes, trying to make up my mind. I found Marshal Johnson, and talked to him for a few minutes.

"Clint, this is Colvin Birch. He's been lookin' for William Thompson for a few weeks, too. Heard he might have some advice for us."

Colvin was an orange-haired young man. He dressed more formally than most. He sat right next to the Marshal, looking very out-of-place.

"I hear that ol' outlaw tried to hang you?" asked Colvin, bluntly.

I was surprised that was the first subject he brought up.

"You're right. He did. I ain't in the bounty business, but I'm going after him for personal reasons. I aim to make it a point you can't get away with killing a Kansan or a Patterson for no reason. I hear there's a lot of other crimes he's committed, too. What are you following him for?"

Colvin snickered.

"I'm gonna catch him and lock 'im up in my basement. I bet his buddies will pay a pretty darned big bounty for him! I'll be rich! And when they come for him, I'll shoot all them bloody rascals!"

"Do you have anyone with you?" I asked. "Or just you?"

"Just me. I'll be more than enough of a match for 'im! I can whip any outlaw!"

"Have you ever shot a gun before?" I asked, suspecting that Colvin was extremely foolish and overconfident.

"No." he replied, embarrassed. His cheeks started to become red. "But I 'spect it ain't too hard."

I stood up, tiring of this redheaded Englishman who was too big for his britches.

"I'll see you later. Good luck. I'll pray for you," I said. To have any chance at all of surviving the Thompson Gang, he would need more than just my prayers.

I walked over to the poker table, which was not very far away from the bar. To my dismay, Bob Peters was arguing with a man dressed in grey. The debate was starting to get very heated.

"I saw you lookin' over my shoulder, Mister! You're cheatin'!" said Bob.
"I did not. And I bet you accuse everyone of cheatin' because you hold
your cards up so damned high!" replied the man.
"If I wanted too, I could cheat damned easy." The man spat on the
ground. Bob took offense.
"You can't get away with cheating in this 'ere establishment! I'll end your
darned winning streak right now!" yelled Bob Peters.
"Y'all quiet down." I said, trying my best to break the fight up. "Just play
a different game, Bob. There won't be no cheats at any of the other
tables. I know because I've been there myself."
Bob didn't care. He was still furious.
"I ain't lettin' him get away with this! Stupid dunce deserves to get shot!
He probably makes his livin' off cheating!"

Things were not getting better. I saw the strangers' hand digging in his
pocket. My heart stopped. I tried to yell Bob's name, but I was too slow.
A half second later, I heard multiple clicks at the same exact time. The
stranger had drawn a Remington derringer out of his coat, and he
pointed it at Bob Peters. Bob was holding his revolver, pointing it back
at the stranger's head. The bartender was aiming a shotgun between both
of the men. A few other men standing around the table had their guns
drawn too.

Things were spiraling out of control. I did not have my gun drawn, and I
prayed I wouldn't get shot at. The tension was unbearable. The
bartender was the first person to take action. He yelled at the arguing
men, angrily.

"Y'all get yourselves outside and settle it out of my saloon! This ain't a
place for shootin'!"
The two men slowly rose out of their seats, with their guns still drawn at
each other.
"Put your guns away this moment, or I'll shoot the both of you!" said
the bartender, still pointing his shotgun.

Bob Peters glanced at me. "If he cheats, you have to shoot him for me, before he shoots you too."

I swallowed hard. Even though I had heard Bob Peters was a good shot, I wasn't sure if he could beat the mysterious man whom he'd accused of cheating.

The man took one of his friends outside, just like Bob Peters. The four of us, plus the bartender exited the saloon. After a few seconds, curious bystanders also left the saloon to get a better look at the action.

"Y'all have done this before, right?" asked the bartender. The two men laughed. They knew what they were doing, even though I personally didn't know the ins and outs of dueling. Honestly, I was pretty darned scared.

Bob Peters walked down the street until he was ten yards from the saloon door. He was right in the middle of the road. His 'cheating' acquaintance did the same. I looked closely at the other man's second. He walked away from the man until he was standing next to the buildings on the side of the street. I assumed this was so he wouldn't be hit by a stray bullet. I did the same.

The bartender threw the man in grey a revolver, so he didn't have to duel with his derringer. He holstered it.
"When I fire this shotgun, the two of you shoot. If y'all miss, there will be another round of shooting if y'all feel like there should be one. Just tell me first. Got it?"
"Yes sir," Bob Peters and the man dressed in grey responded.

My heart went faint. I looked at the two men, with their hands hovering a few inches from their guns. They both shot fire into one another's eyes. I hoped the size of Bob Peters wouldn't get him killed. He was a much bigger target than the thin stranger.

Tense seconds crawled by. The bartender aimed his shotgun up into the sky. It felt like the seconds were turning into minutes. I took a glance at the stranger's second. He looked at me warily. Suddenly,

BOOM! BANGBANG!

Several gunshots whipped my ears like lightning. For a second, it was hard to tell what had happened. I took a look at both of the men. The man in grey was hopping on one foot, falling to the ground. Bob Peters was standing in place frozen, as cold as ice. He holstered his revolver.

"The duel is finished," announced the bartender. "Now, you ain't gettin' back in this bar today, Mister. I don't like these fights going on. Go on to another town and kill someone there." He was slightly insulted.

Bob Peters reluctantly agreed to leave the saloon. The other man was soon carried over to the doctor's office. He had been shot in the leg.

"Did you try to kill him?" I asked, expecting Bob Peters to be mad he wasn't dead.

"Nope. I aimed at his leg on purpose," replied Bob, calmly.

"You are one confusing animal."

"I do know that he won't never be cheatin' again," laughed Bob. "I didn't need to kill him."

CHAPTER 7
Santa Fe, New Mexico, June 26, 1897:

By the time Marshal Lee Johnson stepped out of the saloon, Bob Peters and I were ravenously hungry. It was hard to believe Bob was so hungry since he had just eaten; I, on the other hand, hadn't eaten since lunch. It was now dusk.

We entered the town's hotel, and booked a room to share. Preferring to waste money on gambling and drinks, we did not want to pay the extra costs to purchase separate rooms.

There was food at the hotel, so we indulged in some fairly good buttermilk pie, sausage, and mashed potatoes. For some reason, Bob was hardly fazed by the recent gunfight. He acted like he had not hurt anyone. I decided it would be better not to ask him why.

"How do y'all like Santa Fe?" I asked.
"Ain't too bad, except for the cheaters," said Bob.
"It's average. There's better places in the world," replied Marshal Johnson.
"Marshal, did you hear anything interesting at the bar?"
"I didn't. But I do know where to look next. I'm going to ride off to Catherine James' house tomorrow morning. She might know where he is. Either way, the two of you should go corner Elijah and ask him, too. He might not be keen on saying, but make him tell y'all anyways. Between them two people, I'm sure we'll figure this out."
After the meal, I was stuffed, and I went up into the room. It was getting late.

"Marshal, there's only enough room for two people on the bed. Who's sleepin' on the floor?"

"I think you'll have to, Mister. You're the only one that hasn't been in the bounty business, and I hardly think you've earned your spurs quite yet."

I wasn't about to fight with the Marshal. He had saved my life, anyways. After spending a few uncomfortable minutes getting used to the hard floor, I fell asleep. I dreamed of being back in Kansas, with my mother and old friends…

I heard the sound of something drop on the floor. I awoke with a start. I saw Bob Peters standing on the side of the bed. He had dropped a stone on the floor. I noticed the Marshal had left the hotel already.

"Why'd you do that?" I inquired.
"So you wouldn't try to shoot me," replied Bob.
"Why is that?"
"If someone ever tries to wake you up by shaking you, there's a chance they want something you have. Only safe way to get someone up is by throwin' rocks."
"Makes sense. Where do you think Elijah went to?" I asked.
"Probably either that ol' restaurant, or maybe one of the other places on that there street. Can't think of anywhere else he could have gone to."

Bob and I scarfed down a quick breakfast of eggs and seasoned ham, and departed. We checked the barber, the bank, and a few stores. After we had gotten rid of the alternatives, we checked the restaurant we had visited the day before. Scanning the restaurant, I saw Elijah Denton sitting by the wall.

Bob and I sat down and ordered coffee. After a few minutes, Elijah inexplicably got up and left. I told the waiter we'd be back in a minute for the coffee. We followed Elijah. On a chestnut horse, he trotted away towards the edge of town. He stayed on a small trail heading towards his house, which was presumably not very far away. We hung behind him for a while, until we had spent enough time to be far away from the city.

Bob and I trailed him from about a hundred yards away, careful not to lose him. "As soon as we're far enough out of the town, you ride up on the left. I'll get 'im from the right, and we'll pull guns on him if we need to. Don't shoot him, though. That'll only get us all in trouble. I'll ask 'im where Thompson is headed. Have your lasso ready in case he gets ornery," explained Bob, talking faster than usual, and still slower than most people talk.

We slowly gained some ground on Elijah, and when Bob nodded at me, we galloped up beside him. He was extremely surprised, and sped up to try to get away from us. We stayed at Elijah's side, upsetting his horse. The horse threw his head around angrily.

"Now, tell us where William Thompson went to, and there won't be no bloodshed," shouted Bob, angrily.
"I don't know!" replied Elijah Denton, quickly.
"I know you were partners with him. He probably asked you to rejoin his gang to make it as big as it used t' be. We're gonna shoot you if you don't tell us now," threatened Bob, pulling his gun on the man. Elijah was visibly jumpy.
"I'll tell you. Just don't you shoot me. He rode over here two days ago. He told me he was real mad that I had deserted his gang. He wanted me to get back in it, just like you said. I told him I didn't want no part in killin'. I've been tryin' to live a normal life for a while now. And it was workin' until that Thompson guy came back over here. Yes sir. He meant to shoot me, but I escaped into the town. During the course of the conversation, he told me he was headed towards Grants to try and band with some of his old friends."
"Well that's good information. Now get out of my sights and go back to your house. If I see you head back into town, I'll shoot you," said Bob.

58

We kept on alert until Elijah was two hundred yards away. He must have been real happy to be rid of us.

"Well, that worked well," I announced, proudly.

Bob scowled at me. Apparently, he thought I had done something wrong.

The two of us went back into Santa Fe. After finishing our coffee, we rode over to the hotel. The Marshal arrived at the same time.

"Denton told us Thompson was headed off to Grants," I said.

The Marshal looked distressed. "Catherine told me he was going to Belen! And she didn't look too much like she was lyin'. Someone has to be wrong. Are y'all sure that guy was telling the truth?"

"Let's think for a second," said I. "Who would give better information on where he is? Is either of them defending Bill Thompson and trying to send us out on the wrong trail?"

Bob snorted. "I know Elijah don't care about Thompson, so I could hardly see him lying. But he mighta' thought if he told us the right place, that Thompson would kill him for it. He mighta' lied to protect himself."

"But Catherine used to be his lover. She could have told me the wrong spot to protect him, too. They might still be fond of each other."

"There's a chance of that. Did she say she liked him?" I added.

"Not specifically. I really ain't sure what she thinks of Thompson. They used to be close, but Catherine didn't seem to care too much about him."

"Well I'd say to never trust a woman," said Bob, in disagreement.

"She could have told the truth," replied Lee. "Maybe he came for different reasons, and she doesn't care about him after all."

"Did Catherine seem trustworthy?" I asked.

"About as much as I'd expect. She was never a really predictable person, though."

"Well that settles that," finished Bob. "Elijah Denton had the right place. If anything, he'd prefer Thompson to get killed, and leave him the hell alone."

I still felt very confused. Out of the two places, either one seemed equally viable to me. The only way to tell where Thompson could be was by gut feelings. It had seemed Elijah was honest enough, but there was always the chance he lied to protect himself.

"Either way, we should leave here before Elijah Denton sees us again. He might bushwhack us. You never know with men who used to be outlaws. Can't ever trust 'em," I said.
"Sounds right." replied the Marshal. "We should head down to Albuquerque. From there, there's a path that heads to Grants, and another path that heads to Belen. I'm sure we'll get a better idea once we get there. Our quarry ain't lost just yet."

We rode off on the trail southwards, after stocking up on supplies. The ride was eighty miles, which was two days. We could have made it in one, but that would run the risk of killing or injuring a horse on the way. No matter which direction Thompson had gone, we would be moderately close to him in Albuquerque. Also, he had probably stopped there to restock and rest his horse. We had a very real chance of catching him, as long as someone in Albuquerque knew where he was headed next.

The first day of the trail passed without incident. There was a lot of parched desert on the way. We spent the night at the border of the mountain range north-east of Albuquerque. We heard wolves howling up in the mountains. We decided to keep a guard throughout the night, as bandits were also in the area.

I took the second shift during the night. It was exceedingly hard to stay up. I found myself growing so tired that I had to wake up Marshal Johnson just to stop myself from falling asleep again. I talked with him. He didn't like to talk, because he was tired too, but I explained that it was the only thing keeping me awake.

60

Suddenly, I heard some gunshots off in the distance. I could vaguely see a few muzzle blasts. However, it was so dark, I could not find out anything about what was happening. I kept on alert, holding my new revolver, and hoping I wouldn't have to use it. My breathing became quick.

Marshal Johnson and Bob Peters got up suddenly.
"What's going on?" asked the Marshal.
"Some fight is going on a ways away, on the main trail. It's probably criminals."
"I don't think it's Thompson," replied Marshal Lee. "He's already a day ahead of us, and he can travel quicker alone than the three of us together. Even if it was, we couldn't see him in this darkness."
"That's too bad. My trigger finger is gettin' itchy," replied Bob, laughing.

Although the Marshal had a different opinion, I personally felt that Bill Thompson could be responsible for the gunshots. It was just a hunch, but I knew we were getting closer to them by the hour. We had to cross paths at some time, and now was as good as any.

The sun rose in two hours. The sky became engulfed in orange fire. All of the black mountains were silhouetted against the sky. It was a gorgeous sight to behold.

We rode again towards the southwest, towards the trail to Albuquerque, passing a small forest on the way. My friends talked amongst each other about what had happened when the shots were fired during the night-time. It was unusual for outlaws to strike anyone so late in the night. I realized if we would have stayed on the main trail instead of leaving it for the night, we could have been shot at. It was a close call.

Luckily, our getting out early gave us plenty of time to get to our destination. We didn't need it though, because Albuquerque was only two or three hours away.

I looked at the trail ahead. In front of me was the Marshal. We continued walking our horses. Abruptly, a rabbit ran out from the brush in front of us. As it was halfway across the path, I saw the lightning movement of Marshal Lee's hand. BANG! A flash or fire spat out of the gun. The rabbit rolled away like it had fallen off a steep cliff.

I clapped and smiled. "You ain't nothin' bad, Marshal!"

"Thank you," he replied.

Bob Peters and I waited around silently until the animal was skinned. After that, we headed towards the city of Albuquerque. From there, Grants was four hours away and Belen was two hours away.

I saw some storm clouds out on the horizon, and I felt a bit more wind than usual. The weather seemed to be taking a turn for the worse. Out of nowhere, a big gust of wind swept forcefully through the desert. My horse heard the rustling in the bushes. He reared up on his back legs quickly. I felt a terrible lurch backwards in the saddle, and my right foot fell out of the stirrup. I caught myself on the saddle horn, but I was leaning over to the left. I pulled on the reins, trying to get William under control. It didn't help at all, and actually made things even worse.

William stumbled backwards a few steps, and I would have fallen off if I wasn't hanging onto the saddle horn for dear life. He stayed up for a few seconds. Abruptly, William went back onto his four feet and bolted quickly. He made a sharp turn to the left, and accelerated like a racehorse. I lost my balance as well as my hold on the saddle horn.

I tumbled through the air awkwardly, spinning around twice. All I saw was a whirlwind of blurry color. I felt a huge pound on the side of my body. My head slammed the ground like a beer mug on a table I could just make out the horizon, ground, and a lot of dust from my horse's galloping away.

"Are you alive, Clint?" asked Marshal Johnson, concerned.
I grunted feebly. My ribs hurt like they'd been hit by a nine-pound railroad hammer. I didn't move until I was ready. After about a half-minute, I slowly made it back onto my feet, but my balance was still off. I could hardly walk. My horse was a full fifty yards away from me.

"I'll go get your horse for you. You shouldn't be walking just yet," said Bob Peters. He loped off to where William was standing. Within a minute, Bob and my horse were back.
"Musta' been scared by that big breeze that just went by."
"Darnedawful horse. He's a darned bottle of vinegar sometimes." I sputtered.

I mounted my horse again, and slowly found out that I had no severe injuries. Still, it hurt a lot to ride, and I wanted to get into a town and rest. My ribs would be sore for a while, though. It hurt to move my left arm up or down, and there was a constant background pain in my side. William seemed to be calming down. We kept on the trail to Albuquerque, and my adrenaline slowly faded away. However, the pain remained for many an hour afterwards.

I thought deeply as we walked the horses. It had seemed so simple at first, trying to find Bill Thompson. I was slowly realizing that even though I had two companions, there was always a good chance we could never find the man. There were many different ways our trip could resolve, but I shuddered at the thought of drifting around in New Mexico, following a cold and false trail. A lonely life that would be. The thought of it made me ache for Maddy, and our little old cabin home. I had never been so homesick. Not even during our first weeks in New Mexico, when my heart ached to be back in Kansas.

If there wasn't anyone in Albuquerque to honestly tell us where Bill Thompson fled to, we had a less than half chance of finding him. I hoped we could get some good information.

In a small amount of time, we entered the city. After looking at all the different buildings, the three of us walked into the Sheriff's office. The office was much less tidy than Marshal Johnson's had been in Raton. Sheriff Holman was sitting at his desk, writing something down on a large legal document.

"What's your business?" he asked.
"Marshal Lee Johnson. We are looking for Bill Thompson. Last we heard, he was either in Belen or Grants."
"Here's the 'Wanted' poster," replied the Sheriff, digging through his drawers.
We took a good look at the brand-new, butter colored poster. It had a picture of Bill Thompson's face. It said he was last seen in Grants.
Bob Peters butted in. "I told you not to trust a darned woman! I was right. Men don' lie. We shouldn't have ever gone to Albuquerque in the first darned place."
"She just as well could have told the truth."
"She didn't. Trust me next time. I know what I'm doing," retorted Bob. "I've been in the law for twenty years. I ain't about to take your word for every darned thing."
"Y'all calm it down. Don't spend your time arguing about who thought he was in Grants. You boys have work to do. Now get to it," said Sheriff Holman.

Grants was a short ride across the desert. We left for the trail there after getting some grub at an eatery in Albuquerque. My stomach started to flutter on the trail to Grants. We were getting very close. It was almost time to start talking about tactics, and how to catch the man. I prayed that he hadn't found too many of his friends to initiate into his gang. I knew we were already outnumbered, without him building an even larger gang. We would have to hurry up to catch him in time, before the odds tipped in Bill Thompson's favor.

The odds were in favor of him picking up a good amount of people, so we had to be prepared. I thanked God for my rifle and pistol. The path to Grants was filled with an uneasy silence. Although Bob Peters and Marshal Lee were great shots, it was questionable whether only three people would be enough to catch or kill the man, especially considering his big gang. Bill Thompson had great luck with avoiding bullets, and I doubted it was about to run out now.

After an hour, I saw a few ramshackle buildings off in the distance. Grants was approaching. It seemed like a rather small town, and it didn't look any more interesting than the places we'd previously been to. I personally didn't even consider it a town. It looked more like a village or a little hamlet.

"Good job, William," I laughed. "You almost made it to Grants without hurtin' me. Almost." My side hurt a lot from talking, so I halted and lifted up my shirt. On my left side, there was a good amount of red and purple bruising. I saw a pebble buried in my skin, so I dug around in the wound, trying to dig it out before it infected the cut. Marshal Johnson saw what I was doing, and looked in his saddle bags for something. He handed me a pair of tweezers and a bandage from a little home-made medical kit in his saddle bags.

"Thank you very much," I said. I tended to my wounds, and we entered the town. I felt good enough to do some walking or gambling before bed.

We knew William Thompson was either actually inside the town, or in the immediate vicinity of it. I guessed he was outside the town, because we'd had our little shootout in the countryside instead of the city. It didn't seem like the outlaw was foolish enough to enter many settlements. Everyone for miles around knew his face.

The town was small enough to figure out quickly if Thompson was in it. First, we checked the hotel's waiting room. We booked a room for the three of us. Thompson was not in the front of the hotel, even though it was quite possible that he would have his own room there.

After dropping off some items in our hotel room, the three of us stabled our horses in the barn next to the hotel. The town was so small that the horses were not necessary. We took a look outside the town to get a lay of the land. Following that, we walked over to the town's only restaurant.

The Mexican Cantina was a small place made of adobe. It had some old, beat-up brown chairs as well as a few tables. In the middle of the restaurant, there was a counter and a kitchen behind it. The light entered through a few small windows in the walls. There were some *Mejicanos* as well as Americans eating quietly.

We ordered our food, and found a table in the corner, far away from people. The energy was more tense than usual.

"How are we going to find him?"
"He's probably not out in this town. He has such a big bounty on his head that I doubt he would hang around in the town. I'll bet you some that he's either in the country surrounding here, or even in the town of Gallup. We'll have to zigzag on the trail to Gallup. If we don't find him in the wilderness, he might be in that town," explained Marshal.
"It ain't gonna' be easy to find him, I'll bet. But I'll probably manage it. Least we know where he is. There ain't too many places fer' him to hide. Just the brush-land south of the trail, and the desert north of it. There's a tiny little mountain range north of the trail, too. But that's closer to our destination."
"Sounds like we know what we're doing," I said. I personally didn't have an idea of what they were talking about. They seemed confident and skilled enough to make up for my ignorance of the land, though. I'd

never been further away from Kansas than Raton. All the land we'd travelled was brand-new to me. If our trip was more pleasant, I would have liked to spend more time admiring the scenery.

We made an agreement. We would scour the countryside surrounding the town until it got late, then go into the town to play some faro and sleep. The next day, the three of us could leave the town, and get to Gallup as quickly as possible.

The desert north of the town was flat and vast. It was easy to tell if anyone had been there. With our rifles in hand, we searched the brush land. My stomach started to get damn queasy. I felt our trip nearing its end. I would sometimes aim my rifle at little illusions my eyes created in the landscape. Although there weren't any people around, I constantly saw outlaws moving in the darkness. I took a quick look back at my companions, but they were not half as paranoid as I. They must've been used to this kind of life. We could not find signs of any people. Just as I started to get disappointed, Bob Peters noticed something on the ground in front of him.

"Look 'ere. This was a fire last night. It's darned small. I bet it belonged to Bill Thompson. Only outlaws make such tiny fires. Wait a darned second- who's that?"

A dead body was lying on the ground twenty feet away from the fire. I identified him as Colvin Birch, the Englishman I'd recently met at a saloon. I wasn't surprised he was dead. I felt a twinge of sorrow for him, naïve guy he was.

"That's Colvin Birch. We should bury him," I said.

"We ain't got much time," replied the Marshal, concerned

"I'll just do it quick."

I dug a very shallow grave with a piece of wood from the fire. My companions helped me out, and we were finished within the hour. After saying a quick prayer, we walked away and mounted our horses again.

"This man Colvin is surely one of Thompson's victims. I bet Bill Thompson is probably almost in Gallup by now."

"Maybe not," replied Bob Peters. "He could be biding his time and tryin' to get outta' the newspaper headlines first."
"We did book that hotel room. I think we should stay there and leave at dawn." I added.
"Let's play some damn faro," said Bob.
The Marshal was irritated. "This might be our only chance. Think of the money, Bob."
"Yep. I'll get a lot playin' faro."
"You know what happened last time you gambled. You almost got shot."
"No I didn't," snapped Bob, drawing his revolver but not cocking it.
The Marshal shook his head. "You're gonna regret this."

Back in town, we went to the saloon, gambled, and had some beer. Bob was a big hit at the faro table. He yelled and shouted a lot, and nobody seemed to think he was cheating. Whether he actually was or not, I couldn't say.

I tried a round of 7-card stud horse poker. It was not an easy game. Betting a dollar, I lost half of my chips at first. Then, I had a winning streak that brought me up to a dollar twenty-five. However, I lost ground by overconfident bets. I reduced my betting, but the other players always seemed to get lucky and beat me. Eventually, I got fed up with losing.

I left the table with eighty cents. It seemed like the other players could read my hand like it was facing them instead of me. Frustrated, I decided to join the faro game. It seemed fun, and everyone was talking and laughing. The poker players, on the other hand, were dead serious all the time. I guess the term 'poker face' is correct.

"Ace win, jack lose," said the dealer.
"Gosh darn it!" hollered Bob. He had bet twenty cents on the jack.
I put my chips on the table and played. I seemed to be better at faro than poker. It was, after all, more chance-based than poker. And, it was a lot more fun, especially with Bob at the table.

Ten minutes later, Bob had doubled his earnings, and I walked away with a dollar and ten cents. We'd done well, and we were in very good spirits. We strolled over to the bar to say hello to the Marshal.

"How did y'all do?" he asked.

"I earned a few cents," I replied.

"Fine," said Bob Peters. "I ain't had luck like this in a while."

"Let's hope it doesn't wear off anytime soon. You'll need it if we ever get in range of this posse," said the Marshal.

"So how have you been? Did you meet anyone?" I asked.

"Yep, I did. An old friend of mine moved over here. His name's Jacob Barrows. I used to know him back when I was a Sheriff in Texas. Nice enough guy, although I can't figure out why he would ever move out here."

I heard some fighting going on at the poker table. The shouts easily reached across the whole saloon. Everyone at the bar suddenly dropped their conversation and focused their attention at the poker table.

"Ned Tater, you are one sorry son of a w***re! I saw you pull that ace out of your boot clear as day!" said an angry man dressed in a brown duster.

"No I didn't, Matt! You were imagining things!" yelled another young man.

Please don't tell me this bull crap is starting up again. I'm sick of fights, between this one and that last duel with Bob Peters, I thought.

I looked over at the dispute, reluctant but curious. The excitement of the event drew people in whether they wanted to see it or not. Matt pushed Ned right into the table. He lost his balance, and fell on it, causing a mess of cards to flutter onto the ground. Ned pointed his finger accusingly.

"Well how about that night back in El Paso? Remember that, Matt? You were too drunk to walk! And that wasn't even the worst part!" Ned smiled wickedly.

The look on Matt's face was extremely rage-filled. He spun around and delivered a roundhouse punch to Ned Tater. It glanced off his face, but caused enough damage for his mouth to start bleeding. The blow sent Ned into an enraged fury.

A crowd of people slowly formed around the two men. They were much more curious than me. I had little interest in fighting antics. But the rest of the crowd did, and started to clap. Ned Tater got off the poker table and took a few steps backward. He was still in the fight.

"This ain't done yet, you big stud!" he yelled. Ned spat on the ground at Matt's feet.

Matt took a few steps forward and tried to punch Ned. He missed, and Ned caught his arm. They got all tangled up, pushing against each other.

It looked like they were wrestling. They moved this way and that, until they crashed onto the ground like thunder. The two men struggled and tried to hit each other. A few blows hit, but most of them were weak and glancing. I saw bloody gashes and bruises on both of their faces.

As they brawled brutally, I saw a man run down a flight of stairs. He went over to the fight, and started yelling at Ned and Matt. "Y'all break it up! You've done enough damage to my saloon."

Ned suddenly kicked at the man's leg, and he fell down, too. All three of the men were now on the ground. I could barely understand why Ned was so mad at someone he didn't even know. Matt then grabbed Ned's shirt and started beating on his face with the rage of an angry bull. The owner of the saloon slowly got back on his feet. He had been infuriated by Ned's purposeless kick. He drew a revolver and pointed it right at Ned's bloodied-up face.

"I'm gonna shoot the both of you if you don' stop! Y'all are fightin' like two stallions in the springtime. Get out of here!"

For a moment, the two men stopped to make up their cloudy minds. Although neither man wanted to surrender, they both eventually stood up shakily, and started the long walk towards the entrance of the saloon. A few people stood in between them so they wouldn't hit each other while they were leaving.

I thought the fight was over, but I was soon proven wrong. As soon as they were outside, I heard more yelling and punches being landed. The men still had enough energy and anger left in them to continue the brawl. Some people walked outside to watch the fight, and nobody seemed to care about stopping it. It seemed like they fought for as long outside as inside, and I wondered what they might look like. I hoped they wouldn't die in this ridiculous process. I couldn't help but laugh at how useless the fight was. No matter how the fight would be settled, the fact that Matt had "cheated" would never change.

We waited for a minute until the fight outside was finally over. I never learned who had won, although the two men probably both ended up in the hospital. When the shouting noises and insults finally stopped, I felt ready to talk again to my companions.

"How stupid. I don't get it," I remarked out loud.
"Them men have to settle their differences. They ain't got no other way to do it," said Bob Peters.
"I guess so. But fightin' just ain't right. They should settle their differences on the poker table, or have a drinkin' match or somethin'. Now they're all just in the darned hospital."
Lee Johnson looked at us excitedly.
"I got our confirmation," he said, changing the subject. "The bartender said a man named Bud Thames went through the town yesterday. He seemed suspicious. I'm sure that's just another name for Bill Thompson. Bad news is he had a few friends with him. He ain't gonna be alone. Odds are, if he gets to more towns, he'll recruit even more loner outlaws."

My feelings were mixed. At least we knew where the outlaw was heading. The trail wasn't cold yet. The Marshal and I went back to the hotel. Bob Peters stayed at the casino and played some more faro. I sat on the bed and watched the sun sink under the horizon. I was lucky to have a few moments of respite before tracking down the gang. I tried to enjoy my time, but I felt anxious to get out of the town. Eventually, I drifted asleep, knowing a very important day was ahead of me.

I woke up feeling refreshed but nervous. Luckily, Marshal Lee had let me take the bed for the night. It was only fair. I got ready to head into town. I was the last person up, but my friends had not gotten up much earlier than me. My stomach felt queasy, anticipating what lied ahead.

We prepared for the trip by buying some water and food. On the trail, Bob Peters was an experienced tracker. He quickly discovered that what the bartender had said was true. Four sets of footprints went out of the fire area. They headed towards Gallup, but stayed carefully off the trail and out-of-sight.

We remained in the desert until mountains showed up on the horizon, about an hour later. There were footprints, but no other evidence in the desert. Once we arrived at the mountains, we went southward back to the trail. Bob guessed the gang was going to the same place as the path led to. Also, the horses always had a chance of getting bit by a snake or tripping on a rabbit hole.

There was no one to be seen in the area. Of course, that was not a big surprise. The chances would be that Thompson was already in Gallup on a mission to get more people allied with him. He was still ahead of us by about a day's worth of travel.

It was still early when we reached Gallup. The temperature was not yet eighty degrees. The town was very small, possibly even smaller than Grants. I wondered how often strangers arrived there. It would definitely seem strange to the locals to see the three of us suddenly in town, right after Thompson's Gang. I wondered if the gang actually did stop in a lot of towns we'd visited, or just bypassed them by a few miles. Staying in town seemed like a very risky maneuver to me, especially if Sheriff's offices were in the area.

We skipped our usual ritual of gambling and sleeping, except for visiting a restaurant. The food was not particularly good. I missed the food from Santa Fe.

Marshal Johnson asked the waiter if anyone named Bill Thompson had been in town. The waiter told him that someone named Bud Thames was there, but that was it. He said Bud had just left the restaurant a few hours ago. My heart raced as I pictured how close our adversary was to us. To confirm my suspicion, Marshal Johnson told me that Bud Thames was probably Bill Thompson in disguise.

We didn't waste any time tracking the outlaws, and headed out as soon as we could. Bob discovered quite quickly that they had left the town and gone northwards, on the trail to Colorado. For miles and miles northwards, there was only desert. Even though the desert had small hills, we would still have to be very stealthy to get the jump on the bandits. I knew, however, that the Marshal and bounty hunter would have some tricks up their sleeves.

The tracks were real easy to see. I could identify that about five horses had been travelling. Bob said the tracks were very recent, and that they had probably been made the night before.

As we continued on northward, I felt some aversion to killing Bill Thompson. I had hardly killed a thing in my life before, except a few rabbits and rats. The only man I'd ever killed was the man in the Thompson Gang who had tried to take Patsy Harriot's necklace. And that was purely by happenstance; a self-defense reaction. I didn't plan on it, and didn't necessarily want to do it again.

"Marshal Johnson, are you sure this is the right thing to do? I know we're gonna kill him. We ain't taking prisoners."

Although I expected laughter, the Marshal's response was solemn. "Mister Patterson, I can't tell you if it's right or even legal. I bet Washington's banned bounty hunting already. But I can tell you one thing. A man's got to make his decisions based on what he knows is right, not what people tell him to do. That won't get you nowhere. If you feel he deserves a bullet or two, you should make that choice and go after him. Whether you do help me or not, I'm gonna either shoot or arrest this darned varmint Bill Thompson. He's done enough damage to people, and it's about time his wrongs were made right."

I chewed on what he said. They were wise words. Bob interrupted, speaking suddenly, and quicker than usual.

"How about one of us scouts ahead, and then we dismount and leave our horses here. When they find 'em, we'll shoot 'em. They can't be far away from here."

I was surprised that Bob Peters knew much of anything about tactics. The Marshal disagreed with him. "I think we should ride together with our rifles, and jump them all at once. We could shoot them all dead easily."

"How about you lead my horse, Marshal?" I added. "I'll scout ahead carefully. When I see them, we'll get off the horses and lay on the ground. Maybe that rifle of yours will be as nice to us as it usually is. If they find us too quick after the ambush, we'll ride away and shoot from there."

Marshal Johnson nodded, pleased. Bob wasn't, however.

"No. We'll be more obvious than a tree in a cornfield if we have to catch up with you. I think you should do the shootin' and layin', Marshal. We'll stay behind."

Marshal Johnson thought about the plan. "The best idea is for me to distract them, and pick off a few with my rifle. Y'all can gallop around me and flank them. Since there's all these little hills, they probably won't notice y'all. One of us will surely get a clean sweep at them. Once you flank them, they'll be surrounded. But I ain't tryin' to make them surrender. We're outnumbered here. They'll know that. If they do surrender, we can stop shootin'. But I'll bet you they won't. Odds are we'll have to kill them or injure them bad enough that they'll wanna be in Heaven. Not like they ever will be," he laughed.

I nodded in approval. Surprisingly, so did Bob Peters. I was pleased we were finally at a consensus. Now the only problem was actually killing the outlaws, which was easier said than done. I could feel the stress of being outnumbered.

"We better get going. They're probably on the move right now. I know they have a habit to start travelling around this hour," said Bob.

We walked our horses slowly. Marshal Johnson was in front of us by about five yards, with his big buffalo rifle in hand. Bob Peters and I were slightly to the left of the Marshal. We walked up to the top of a ridge. My stomach felt fluttery. The tension was starting to become intense.

"See anything?" I asked.

"I thought I might have seen the top of a hat up there. I can't tell for sure." The Marshal whispered. He listened carefully for sounds. I couldn't tell if he heard anything. We walked to a small valley before the next ridge. I had a feeling the gang was on the top of the ridge.

"Stay back here," whispered the Marshal. "As soon as you hear a shot, gallop in from the left side and flank them."

"You found them?" I asked. My question wasn't answered.

The Marshal dismounted and left his horse in the valley. He crouched down and slowly walked to the top of the hill. Once he was at the top, he laid down. I waited in anticipation. The moment had finally come. Each second felt like it lasted minutes.

 BOOM!

CHAPTER 8
New Mexico, June 28, 1897:

I saw a ball of fire jump out of Marshal Lee's rifle. The sound was so loud my ears hurt. I heard yelling and shouting from on top of the ridge. Another, less loud gunshot followed the shot from the Marshal's rifle. It missed him by a hair. Marshal Johnson instinctively moved away from the bullet and looked back at where it had gone. I saw desperation in his eyes.

Bob Peters was already heading towards the outlaws. I kicked William into a gallop and followed as closely as I could. The outlaws were positioned in a plateau at the top of the ridge. The set up a camp, and were about to go out northwards, towards Colorado. As we galloped, we stayed on the slope to avoid getting shot at. I could barely see the outlaws. They seemed to be occupied with shooting at the Marshal. I hoped they were missing. I clenched my teeth together and prayed the shots were missing him. I tried to look back, but I couldn't see Marshal Johnson.

The two of us kept riding until we were past the outlaws, then we spun around, and faced them. We were about thirty yards away. I heard a lot of shooting going on. The posse was ten feet above us, right at the top of a steep incline.

I hope they didn't see us riding around them, I thought.

I rode up to a point where I could see the outlaws. There was only one body on the ground. I saw the four other outlaws still standing. I couldn't tell which man had been killed.

I saw Bob Peters pull out his rifle, and I did the same. I took my Winchester out of its scabbard, trying my best to line up the front and back sights. I cycled the lever and drew a bead on one of the men. They did not notice I was there.

BANG! The bullet hit the ground at an outlaw's foot. I chambered another round quick as lightning. BANG! The same man spun around and hit the ground. I smiled. He was shot in the leg. I felt guilty to shoot the man already on the ground, so I hesitated for a second.

The remaining three men turned around to shoot at me and Bob. I felt a bullet fly right next to my head. A second after, one whizzed right past the side of my horse. William reared up. I barely managed to stay in the saddle. If I didn't have the practice of William just rearing up the day before, I probably would have fallen off. William was getting extremely nervous. I watched Bob Peters gallop right up to the outlaws, out of the blue.

What in darned hell is he doing? I thought. *He is crazy! We never told him to do that! What a stupid idea!*

The Marshal had ceased shooting a few seconds before, and I wondered why. I hoped he hadn't been shot.

"What the damn hell are you doing?" I yelled. I was never answered. As Bob Peters rode by the outlaws, he fanned his revolver at them. The six shots all sounded like one to me. The bullets tore through the remaining outlaws. One of the wounded man was shot dead by the sudden volley. Also, one of the outlaws who hadn't been shot yet got a bullet through the chest. He quickly collapsed onto the ground.

I heard another shot, followed by a puff of grey smoke from an outlaw's rifle. Suddenly, Bob's black horse was running alone. Behind the horse laid the body of my friend. I gasped. I felt sickened and disgusted. Rage swelled up inside my heart at the man who'd shot Bob Peters.

Aiming my rifle at one of the remaining men, I chambered another cartridge. BANG! I worked the lever again. BANG! BANG! BANG! I shot all the remaining cartridges until my rifle was unloaded. Most of the shots had hit their target.

All of the outlaws were on the ground. I let out some air. The unbearable stress of the shootout had stifled my breathing. I dismounted William, drew my revolver, and slowly walked up to the men.

The closest man to me was the one who'd shot Bob off his horse. He was now a ravaged mess, due to me. I guiltily averted my eyes. I couldn't stand looking at him. The second man was in the same shape. He had been killed by Bob during his wild run.

The third person was shot in the chest. He was dying slowly, but definitely on his way out. He sputtered some incoherent nonsense.

I found the fourth man a few feet from the third. He'd been shot by Marshal Johnson's rifle. I could tell that because there was a huge hole in his back near his heart. It had obviously been from a buffalo rifle. His face was forever frozen in a look of surprised disbelief.

The final outlaw was Bill Thompson himself. I realized he was one of the men the Marshal had shot with his rifle. His leg had a huge, bloody hole in it. Bill Thompson was hurt, but there was still a chance he would survive the ordeal.

I thought for a second about Bill Thompson's bounty. The poster had said 'WANTED DEAD OR ALIVE'. Either way would give me the same amount of money. I moved my hand over to my rope, considering tying him up and bringing him back alive.

Images of my attempted hanging and robbery flooded my head. My heart burned. Did he deserve being put in some jail and released years afterwards? What if he escaped? The only way to make sure justice was served was to kill him on the spot.

I cocked my revolver, aiming at the gunslinger's chest. I took a deep breath. I thought about how displeased my mom would be if she saw me there.

"This is what you would have done to me, worthless thumb-suckin' horse-stealin' man-killin' varmint," I said, quite quietly and not really meaning it. I laughed a bit, considering that was exactly what he had called me a week before. The tables were turned, and I finally had the upper hand.

I cocked the revolver, and looked right in Bill Thompson's eyes. The gun felt heavy in my hand, and I felt my sweaty finger on the trigger. But then I felt a pang of mercy in my heart. I suppose you could call it 'conscience.' I had come all this way, worked so hard to get to this moment of glory. And I couldn't shoot the man. I just wasn't a stone-cold killer like Bob Peters or the man right in front of me. I decocked and lowered my revolver to give him mercy. Then, I saw his hand twitch. Bill Thompson quickly drew his revolver, trying to surprise me. I saw a flash of light reflecting off the man's six-gun, pointed straight at my face.

I knew this was the end for me.

BANG!

For a second, I didn't know what had happened. I felt my body reel from some sort of impact. Then I looked down and saw Bill Thompson's body bent backwards, onto the ground. There was a hole in his chest, slowly gushing out blood. I sighed and holstered my revolver. I was safe.

A distance away, I saw a puff of smoke from the Marshal's rifle. He killed Bill Thompson.

Marshall hooped in glee, "Yeeehaw! Revenge is sweet!" he hollered gaily. I wished I could join him in his excitement, but I felt more like a dog with his tail tucked between his legs. I wasn't cut out for killing like Bob Peters was. He had no qualms about it. To him, it was a way of life. That wasn't me.

I walked back to my horse. He was quite a distance away from the outlaws. I saddled up and trotted William back to where the Marshal had shot his rifle. I prayed he wasn't dead. Marshal Johnson was hunched over on the ground awkwardly. I saw blood on the ground. I gasped, dismounted, and ran over to him.

"Marshal! Marshal! Are you shot?"

I heard a small grunt from the man. He slowly rose to his feet. I saw blood staining his shirt, right on the side of his hip.

"I'm shot. But I'll survive." he replied, slowly and painfully. There was a smile on his face telling me that his wound wasn't so severe. I assisted the Marshal in the lopsided walk over to his horse. With his good leg, he could mount the horse.

"Can you ride?" I asked, doubtful.

"I'll manage. But don't go fast. It hurts like gettin' stung by a hive full of bees."

We rode over to the spot where Bob Peters had been shot down. He was not alive. My eyes averted his body. I felt a heart-wrenching pang of guilt. I hadn't stopped him from galloping away. If I hadn't been getting shot at in that exact moment, I probably could have saved Bob's life.

"That's too damn bad," said the Marshal, his head bent to the ground. "Sorry, I can't help you bury him."

"How can I bury him without a shovel?" I asked, confused.

"You'll have to tie him to your saddle and take him into town. And tie that Thompson man to my saddle."

I did as the Marshal instructed. We were on the way back to Gallup within ten minutes. I tied up Bob Peter's horse and led him with a rope. The ride back felt just as long as the ride away from Gallup, but for

82

different reasons. While the ride out was slow and suspenseful, the ride back to Gallup was slow and slightly dismal. Keeping two bodies on our horses, and leading an extra horse confined us to a very slow pace. Even if we didn't have an extra burden, I would have rode slowly anyways. The adrenaline rush from the fight wore off and left me in a slump.

When we reached the town, I felt like we had traveled for many miles. As we arrived, all the locals stared at us wide-eyed and amazed. They probably had the misconception that the two of us had brought in two outlaws for bounty; instead of the reality of the two of us bringing in one outlaw, and one lifeless friend.

As the barber dressed Marshal Johnson's wound, I took Bob Peter's body over to the small church to be buried. I said a prayer for him, and thanked him for helping us in the fight. I had noticed my horse getting fatigued from carrying his heavy body. It was in William's best interest for Bob Peters to be buried. However, I felt very unhappy to say goodbye to Bob for the last time. My heart ached.

I asked around to see if anyone wanted Bob Peter's horse, since it would be difficult to lead him all the way back to Raton. I eventually found a buyer. An old cowboy named Billy Reeds needed a heavy horse like Bob's for pulling his tiller. He paid a modest price of ten dollars for the gelding.

At this point, my trip felt complete. I was relieved to be heading back home, towards my loving wife. In my wildest dreams, I had not expected a journey like that.

We stayed in town for a few more hours, so the Marshal got some time to rest for the long journey back. The bullet had missed his major organs, so he recovered quickly. Still, he would have to wear a bandage on his leg for several weeks.

After getting some food at the restaurant, we departed for Grants. My horse was happy to be carrying two hundred pounds less. I noticed that he was starting to calm down with all the miles he'd taken me. Although there were a few objects on the way back that should have scared him, he didn't seem to really care. I didn't care about too much at that point either. All that mattered was- we were finally going home.

CHAPTER 9
Grants, New Mexico, June 29, 1897:

We arrived in Grants the day after the shootout. Our horses had shared the burden of Bill Thompson's dead body for such a long time that they were becoming tired. Since there was a Sheriff's office in Grants, we gave the body away and obtained a note of shipment for the bounty money. Since there wasn't any place in the town that had such a large sum of money, we would have to wait awhile to receive it.

As I walked out of the office, I saw a man who looked like he had been licked badly. His arm was in a cast, his lip was split, and his face was bruised and discolored like a faded "wanted" poster.

I heard a man standing a few feet away from me whisper that the man was Ned Tater. I was honestly surprised he had survived the fight at the saloon. It seemed like a fight to the death at the time.

"Where's that guy Ned's partner Matt?" I asked the stranger.

"He's in the hospital. He can't walk right now. He might recover, but I ain't sure. He ain't his partner, though. Were you in the saloon on that night? You should know."

"Yes sir. My Lord, what a crazy fight. I ain't never seen somethin' like it," I replied.

"I know." said the man. "It was purty fun to watch, though." He laughed lightly. "I've seen a few, but that fight had to be one of the best."

"Dang. Well, I guess someone won that fight. I just hope they don't get into another one. That wouldn't be no good," I replied.

After staying in town somewhat longer to stock up and eat, we made the long trip back to Raton. The Marshal and I discussed many a time what we had thought of the shootout. Lee Johnson regretted the fact the he hadn't found some cover to hide in between shots. He acknowledged the fact that he easily could have been killed if the outlaws had better aim. Luckily, we had the element of surprise in the fight.

I, on the other hand, had my own regrets. Bob's death could have been avoided, if he hadn't been so foolhardy. Although I felt it was partially my fault he died, the Marshal pointed out that he'd made his own decision without telling any of us beforehand. There was nothing we could have done to save him.

As we rode towards Raton, I saw some familiar landmarks I'd first seen on the ride away from the town. I felt like I was finally going back to somewhere I knew and loved. The bounty hunting trip had been too long, although I knew I would always look back fondly at all the faro, blackjack, drinks, conversation, and interesting places along the way.

I pondered the necklace. If Josiah hadn't told me the story about it, I never would have left the house in the first place. So many things could have turned out differently; I could have been shot by the first outlaw I saw. I could have been hanged, or killed in the shootout. Luck was with me that I was still alive and well. The cards had been stacked against me. I noticed, surprised, that I was the only one to emerge from the fight without a scratch. It took some getting used to, since I never considered myself anywhere near as good a shot as Bob Peters or Marshal Johnson. If anything, I would have thought I'd be the one killed in the fight. If not me, it would have been the Marshal, not Bob Peters, one of the best bounty hunters in the state.

The town grew and grew in size, until I was suddenly back in good old Raton. I hitched my horse outside the Sheriff's office, and walked into the office with Marshal Johnson. Saying goodbye felt strange, since I had grown to know him so well over the course of the trip.

We walked into the office. The Marshal sat down at his desk. He dug around in his desk for a while and took out a bottle of Jack Daniels. He poured us a shot, as usual.

"Mister Patterson, thanks for helping us out. I wouldn't have done so well without you. I probably would have got shot to death. Now, I am getting old. I aim to get out of Raton darned soon. I'm gettin' sick of it here. I got plans to go down to Texas with my wife. Now that I got all this money. I know I told you I'd give you your fair share, but that was only if you killed William Thompson."

"That ain't true," I replied, steadily. "You said the money would be mine if I helped you capture him. And that's what I did. I caught the guy. You shot him."

Marshal Johnson shook his head.

"Are you kidding? I shot him. Did you see that big ol' hole in Bill Thompson's side or not? I need that bounty money. Sure I would of given it to you if you'd been the one to actually shoot him!"

"I captured him! I was standin' right in front of his darned body. You would never have had a chance to shoot him, had it not been for me. I got to him first! You said that was part of the deal! Besides, you never said it mattered who actually shot him."

"You had your chance to shoot him, you were staring him stone-cold in the eyes. But for some godforsaken reason – you refused. Now give me that invoice, please."

"Damn you, stupid Marshal," I hissed. Marshal Johnson looked like a lazy cheater as he sat with his feet on the table.

"I bet you think you're somethin' real special? If you ain't givin' me that paper, I'll take it from you," Marshal threatened.

I wasn't about to shoot Marshal Johnson. As angry as I was at him, I didn't have much of a choice. I took the invoice out of my pocket.

"Here you go. Have a nice day," I said, bitterly. I put the paper on the desk. I spat on the ground as I walked out of the Sheriff's Office.

I leaned on the wall of the Sheriff's office, feeling disappointed. I was sure at least some of the money would be mine. My horse looked up at me and nickered softly. I walked up to him. I felt my ribs, and noticed they were starting to become less sore.

"William, you've been a good horse. Thanks for not acting like a bronco, except for that one-time incident on the trail. You've settled down a lot since before this trip. And I ain't mad at you for rearin' up when those bullets were comin' at us. I would have done the same thing if I were a horse."

He stared at me understandingly. I scratched his forehead, which he seemed to like. After a few minutes, I saddled up and rode out of town. Luckily, there were no outlaws along the way. Bill Thompson's gang was gone forever.

The only real concern I had was, where had Patsy Harriot's necklace ended up? I personally suspected it had ended up in the hands of some outlaw or treasure seeker before me. Then again, there was always a good chance she had never worn the necklace into the cave in the first place. I realized I had never actually searched William Thompson's body. I had been too repulsed by the whole incident to touch him afterwards. He easily could have had the necklace in his pocket. If he did, I'd lost my chance to get the treasure. The Sheriff's Department would find it once we gave them the body. Marshal would win again. Although I was frustrated, there was could be nothing good about regretting the past.

The trail back home was relaxing and familiar. It felt a whole world safer without the Thompson Gang in the area. I remembered how it had felt when they pervaded the area. Any sort of travel felt life-threatening.

In about an hour, I reached my destination- the Patterson Ranch.

"Maddy?" I asked.

In a moment, my wife came running out of the kitchen. I saw a big smile on her face. I'd never seen her happier since the day I met her.

"Clint! you're back! You're back!" she walked up to me and gave me a hug and kiss. A long slow kiss. "Thank God you're alive!"

"I've been around. We went all the way to Gallup, lookin' after Bill Thompson. We found him there. Thank you for waiting for me. I know it ain't easy being out in the desert alone."

"I wasn't sure you'd make it back. I was worried sick about you."

"Well thanks for being so concerned. I know myself-- it wasn't a safe trip."

Maddy looked up at my hat.

"Where'd you get that big old feather?" she asked.

"A vulture. I shot it with Marshal Johnson's buffalo rifle."

"Wow! Never thought you'd be such a great shot. It looks nice in that hat."

"Thanks. I have some good news for you," I said, hopefully.

"What is it?" she asked, curious.

I wished at that moment I could tell her about the bounty. I wanted so much to give her that bounty. But here I was, coming back with nothing. Not even man enough to shoot a worthless varmint.

"I captured Bill Thompson," I said weakly. "And Marshal shot him. And I might as well just tell you right now – Marshal ain't givin' me a damn cent of the bounty money," I said, exasperated.

"Oh Clint, that is best news! That is what I was hoping you would say!"

"What?" I asked, stunned. I felt certain she would be disappointed in me.

She continued, "I'm so glad that vile man has been put to rest…. And I'm even happier you weren't the one to do it! I don't care about any damn bounty money! I care more about you. You ain't a killer. That's not you. And I always I knew that. But you had to learn for yourself. I'm just glad you're back home." I noticed her eyes were gleaming with tears, and her smile was shining softly.

And then at that moment, I saw something else shining. A glint around her neck—a gleam as bright as a ray of sun, and as shiny as the Marshal's badge.

What the heck? I thought.

"Maddy, what is that around your neck?" I inquired.

"Oh, it's just…a necklace…I … sort of… just… found it," she stammered.

"How the darned heck did you find that?" I asked, amazed. I could hardly believe what I saw. There was no doubt, that was it! Patsy Harriot's necklace was right in front of me, and it was beautiful. I never thought I would ever see it.

"Well if I told you, you'd never believe me. Heck, I wouldn't even believe myself!"

After all I just went through; I didn't think there was anything that would surprise me. "Try me," I said.

"You promise you won't laugh…"

"At you? I won't never laugh at you."

"And you won't think I'm crazy either?" she added.

I shook my head. "Probably not."

"Well, on Thursday night, I had the darndest time sleeping. I felt like there was some storm or energy making me think about scary things. Tossing and turning, feeling sheer fear. I found myself worried sick about you. After hours, I finally fell asleep. And I had a very striking dream. More vivid than I ever dreamt before. It felt real…

"I dreamed of this young girl– a teenager actually. I could just make out her silhouette. I don't know where I was. She said to me, '*Your husband is going to be all right. He is a good man and he made the right decision. He has finally brought me to rest.*' And then she told me that there was a treasure waiting, as a reward, for YOU, Clint. She gave me specific instructions on where to find it.

"The next morning, I doubted the whole dream. But I just couldn't get it off my mind. So after a while, I decided to follow the girl's instructions, as crazy as they sounded," she gave a nervous laugh. "I traveled for a long time, all the way to the place she wanted me to go. It was a big cave. She'd mentioned a very specific rock. I found the rock, and it was exactly as she described it. I lifted it up, with all my strength. Then I crawled into the dim cave, and just sitting there, was this necklace! It was right on the ground in front of me, as if it had been placed there just for me."

My mind was racing… I thought back…Thursday night, Thursday night, that was the night of Maddy's dream. That was the night Bill Thompson died.

Maddy didn't even know about Patsy Harriot! She was in the kitchen while Josiah told his long story about the necklace and the story behind it.

A flood of thoughts rushed through my mind so powerful in their force that they almost knocked me over. The legend of Patsy Harriot. The journey. The sheriff. Bill Thompson. My conscience. And now my beautiful wife standing there with a glistening necklace. A vision of Patsy Harriot. Avenging her death. Bringing her to rest.

I had just been given all the riches in the world. Did she have any idea what this necklace was worth or how our life was about to change? We could buy just about anything we wanted to.

She must have noticed me, about to reel. "Are you okay? What are you thinking?" she asked me.

I couldn't even begin to explain. Not now. There was too much rushing through my head like a river. The only thing I could do was wrap my arms around her, and hold her tight. She was my rock, and I had finally come home.

-THE END-